THE DREAMLIFE OF BRIDGES

The Dreamlife
of Bridges

ROBERT STRANDQUIST

ANVIL PRESS | VANCOUVER

CANADIAN CATALOGUING IN PUBLICATION DATA
Strandquist, Robert Arthur, 1952-
The dreamlife of bridges

ISBN: 1-895636-46-9
I. Title
PS8587.T6789D73 2003   C813'.6   C2003-910942-6
PR9199.4.S77D73 2003

Printed and bound in Canada
Cover design: Rayola Graphic Design
Typesetting: HeimatHouse

Represented in Canada by the Literary Press Group
Distributed by the University of Toronto Press

The publisher gratefully acknowledges the financial assistance of the B.C. Arts Council, the Canada Council for the Arts, and the Book Publishing Industry Development Program (BPIDP) for their support of our publishing program.

The Canada Council | Le Conseil des Arts
for the Arts | du Canada

BRITISH
COLUMBIA
ARTS COUNCIL
Supported by the Province of British Columbia

Anvil Press
P.O. Box 3008, Main Post Office
Vancouver, B.C. V6B 3X5   CANADA
www.anvilpress.com

For Chris Petty

with thanks to
Brian Kaufman, Jenn Farrell
and Lisa Sweanor
for their patience and support

Over the old wooden bridge
no traveller
crossed.
—Thoreau

One

DISTRACTED AND HUNGRY LOOKING, Leo leans on the counter and watches people in the mall. Through multifarious layers of glass and chrome the kaleidoscoping female form, broken up and recombined, stirs him with its camber and concave, its turning around stillness.

In the window of the shop is a display of shoes suspended by wires a few inches above the floor. Hanging from the ceiling are a bowler hat, a baseball cap, and a flowered wedding crown. As if to complete the social environment there floats a martini glass, a beer mug, and an unlit cigar at about gossip level. Joe, Leo's nimble boss, was the one who came up with the idea.

An average savage stops to gape at the display, and mouth banalities for the benefit of the children hanging from his belt. Leo goes into the back and pours himself a cup of coffee. He returns to find a woman struggling with the heavy glass door, trying to manoeuvre a stroller through. Leo watches without pity, hypnotized by her fairytale colour scheme, and the stroller, which is done up like a float in a parade, carrying two perplexed white geese.

I need to see the shoemaker, the woman says, more dignified than quixotic. She's in a soft yellow velveteen dress and has a big violet bow in her snow blonde hair.

Is that so? Leo says, safely behind the counter, searching her face for signs of insanity.

He guesses her age to be somewhere between fifty and seventy, yet nothing seems old about her. Though her seriousness belies the general impression.

It's Little One, her feet, she says, stroking the birds' necks.

Have you tried the pet store? he asks, watching her hands.

Have you been in one of those places?

Ducks Unlimited? he tries.

Inquisitive and amused by his uncertainty, she lifts the roasting-pan-sized creature onto the counter. *Show the nice man your feet,* she says.

Do birds have feet? he asks her, unnerved by the sensual power of its wings.

I thought booties, she says.

Why me? he asks the ceiling, hoping to insult her just enough so she'll go away.

When your children needed shoes, you made them

shoes, am I correct? Her accent surfacing, Slavic and frustrated.

I've never made a shoe in my life, Leo confesses.

As you can see, her situation is acute.

Let me get this straight, we're talking about a . . . bird?

How much do you know? Would you like to tell us all how much you know? she says, referring to the customers and bystanders who have come into the store, attracted by the birds.

If it walks like a duck, and quacks like a duck . . .

My girls don't think they're birds. And don't you think they'd be the ones to know?

A couple of old men nod, apparently in agreement.

What are they then? Leo asks.

If you were raised by goats, you'd probably think you were a goat, she says.

I'm not a goat.

And not the shoemaker. Can I speak with him . . .

Jean-Paul isn't here anymore.

Well, you can see my problem then.

He looks at her mouth. Her tongue is translucent, shimmering like soft porcelain.

Indeed, he says, *I can.* He thinks of his retired mentor, how he would have known how to handle this situation.

She doesn't like pigskin, she says, encouraged by his silence.

Who does?

You don't know how much this means to us.

On the slippery slope of assent and not sure how he got there, Leo opens the photocopier tray for a sheet of paper, something to trace the bird's feet on. The quickest way out of any situation is to go along with it. But he has a better idea and gets her to put the bird up on the photocopier glass.

Come back in a month and we'll see, he tells her as he examines the reproduction of feathers and webbed feet.

A month? wonders another interested party.

The poor thing can't wait that long, says another.

The pavement is so hot.

Leo smirks.

Sure, okay, a week then. He knows when he's cornered.

He holds the door open as if they are a royal procession, with everybody in the mall watching.

Say thank you to the nice people, the bird woman says, waving her gloved fingers, clownish and subtle. He watches for a while as she makes her way through the mall, where she stops frequently to annoy people.

Joe is self-taught. He takes people's ugly feet in both hands and never misses a chance to expound on his knowledge of biomechanics. Most of what he's learned has been through trial and error. He gets them to walk up and down the showroom floor while he studies their gait. They climb into his examination chair so he can study the soft tissue of their feet.

When Joe gets back from lunch Leo returns to his work in the lab. He slits the thin membrane of adhesive between the crepe sole and the white latex tread of a name brand running shoe, blocking everything else from his mind.

The runner lain open, its tread separated from the sole, he looks through his inventory of sheet stock crepe and rather than cut into a new piece of the six millimetre he decides to use two scraps of three mil. They differ slightly in shade, but Leo's sight is colour poor and he doesn't catch it right away. He traces the right sole onto both pieces and applies a thin coat of Barge cement to the relevant surfaces.

Untying his apron he drops it among the clutter on his bench—a ball stretcher, hammers, tins of polish, and a coffee-ringed *Playboy* calendar he keeps track of his appointments on. He means to tidy up when business slows down, to organize the sticky drawers, sort the brass nails from the steel ones, the thousands of objects he'll never have a name for. Against the wall are a couple of ancient sewing machines, unused since Jean-Paul retired. He was a cobbler from the old school with breathtaking skill, and he handled the cumbersome, idiosyncratic machines like they were his wives.

In the bathroom Leo feels the cold kiss of the plumbing when he lowers his weight to the toilet. He peruses a catalogue from a stack on the frosted window's ledge, one selling herbal remedies. He's had diarrhoea for months and none of the experts know why. It started around the time his son killed himself, though he doesn't think the two are connected. Standing at attention in the mirror makes his lumbar ache.

When the glue is tacky he turns the two pieces into one, and with it builds a six-millimetre rise into the shoe, shaping it on the sanding belt and then reattaching the tread. He cleans it up on the drum sander and puts it beside its mate along with the work order on the outgoing shelf.

Behind the mall, after work, he picks up the trail for his half-hour walk home which takes him between the brewery's chain-link fence and the rail yard siding where a couple of boxcars have been wasting gravity for the past week. Their proximity to the path is disconcerting and the perfumes of creosote and oil shadow him with memories of childhood. It was rare to see rolling stock this far inside the spread of condos along False Creek.

He sometimes hears the whistle at night, if the atmospheric conditions are right, the warning blasts carrying for miles across the city, as the train makes one crossing after another, down from MacKenzie Heights, passing Thirty-seventh Avenue, Thirty-third, Sixteenth, Twelfth, Seventh, Fourth, the engineer

pulling lightly on his horn, sensitive to the neighbour-
hoods he haunts.

As a boy, Leo flattened nails and killed reptiles
under the swaying boxcars that paraded daily behind
his Etobicoke fence; but now, middle-aged in La-La
Land, his heart beats rapid as a rat's if he's hiking the
cut and hears one coming.

He pauses under the Burrard Bridge, as he does most
days. With the imbecile gods drumming overhead, and
the arching bridge columns providing the illusion of an
uninterrupted cathedral, it is all made surreal and pure
by the unexpected surfeit of light. At its apex, the long
bridge achieves a height sufficient to clear the masts of
ships and gives suicides a better than fifty-fifty chance.
It holds a preoccupied silence, a minute-by-minute
refuge from the importance of things.

What's left of a utility bunker that once stood here,
is a staging area for dust motes, a flatness waiting for
a carpenter's level. Today its sole possessor is a doll, a
matryoushka doll. Leo hasn't seen one of these in
years. It seems lost, out of place. He twists it apart, his
desire for meaning inflating disproportionately with
each smaller duplication of the babushka's face. He
finds it irritating, yet at the same time he wants to take
it home, but he's gotten superstitious of late and is
careful to leave it exactly as he found it.

When he's nearly home, Leo realizes he can't locate his keys. He must have taken them out for some reason at work or they fell out under the bridge when he stopped to look at that doll. The kitchen window jams at the one-by-two he secured it with this very morning and the furnace room window is sealed tight with old paint.

He goes around to the front of the house and up the stairs, pressing the button with his thumb. Getting this close to his new neighbour for the first time he notices the frayed sleeves of her expensive blouse. Under a skillful layer of make-up is a woman older than he at first thought. A few times her Barbie doll legs had scissored past his face in the flowerbed window. Last night he was eavesdropping at the adjoining stairs, fascinated by the ineffectual charm of the woman, up against her three-year-old son. Now he was hoping he'd forgotten to lock the bottom door.

Just a minute, she says into the phone, looking down at Leo.

There's a door, he says, *in my suite; stairs, I think, between your place and mine. In the kitchen perhaps. Do you mind if I just have a look?*

Who are you? she asks.

I'm your neighbour, he says.

You're the guy downstairs?

I don't have my key.

Just don't make a habit of it, she says awkwardly, letting him in.

It's never happened before. I swear.

He slips past her into a sea of toys where the frowning three-year-old is standing, looking lost. The boy follows Leo to the kitchen and tells him the light is burned out in the staircase. Leo winks at him, and the boy grins at the same time he's trying to suppress it.

Darkness wobbles in the staircase and there's a scent of the outdoors lingering in the overcoats hanging there. He goes down and checks the door. It was worth a try.

As he turns to go back up, he sees the boy holding the door, arm out like a gunslinger.

Bye bye, he says and flings it closed.

A mop, a witch's broom, registers the moment before he is sealed in darkness. And before he can get to the top step he hears the bolt clatter shut. Leaning on the door he can feel the heat of the boy on the other side.

Come on kid, it's dark in here.

Buried alive in the nightmare of a child, a fear that even in the grave you were justly terrified, that peace was damned from the first. He was in there for a couple of sweaty minutes before the boy's mother opened the door. They stared at each other long enough to see that there was nothing much of interest for either of them.

She remembers a key on a shoelace somewhere and begins a disorganized search. Leo watches her worry through kitchen drawers, but he needs to get outside so he can think straight. A solution exists to every problem, otherwise where would the problem have originated? All it required was time and a lot of quiet.

He walks around the yard accusing his pockets, searching between the bricks of the uneven path to his basement suite door. It was really beginning to bother him, the thought of the inconvenience, either of breaking in or trying to locate the owner. As he runs these things through his mind he discovers them, hanging there like testicles in the lock of the door to his suite.

He goes to explain it to his neighbour, whose name he learns is June, and she says to the boy as he clings to her leg: *Did you hear that Gummy Bear? They were in his door all along.*

Memory, he says, tapping his skull, *who needs it?*

Why don't you come up for dinner sometime?

Leo is surprised. *Yah, sure, love to. When?*

How about tomorrow?

Finally into his evening, Leo stares out the front window and watches his neighbours dash from their cars to their front porches as though snipers were hiding in the trees.

Overhead the boy starts hammering and Leo goes numb and slips into the blackness of memory. When he flew back east for his son's funeral he had to run the last mile to the cemetery. He stood with his in-

laws in the rain, earnestness wrapping him up. He was
the last to arrive at the graveside, but was the one who
was wishing the hardest, the one who could still catch
his falling child and pull him back, because somehow
he knew there must still be time.

Next evening, Leo goes through the medicine chest
and his night table looking for the condom that's never
there when you need it. He calculates the distance to
the nearest drug store against the possibility that anything could happen with that kid around.

He rings the bell with his middle finger for confidence but when June answers in an astonishing red
blouse and black skirt he can't think of anything to
say. She asks him if he wants a glass of wine and
apparently doesn't hear his *no thanks*, returning from
the kitchen with an empty wine glass. The toys have
been bulldozed into a pile and Gunther is playing
with a doll on the couch.

I need to tell you something, she says.

He can see that she's distracted, thinking maybe
something important has come up.

I shouldn't have told him you were coming over,
she says, trying to be delicate but just being vague. *It's
all a game to him.*

Leo puts the glass down on the wicker coffee table.
He has no idea what she's talking about.

He's done it before, she says, returning to the
kitchen.

What?

You don't want to know how many times.

Leo picks up the doll he thought the boy was finished playing with.

That's mine, says Gunther, snatching it back.

Is that Wonder Woman? Leo says, remaining civil.

Mine.

Why do they call her Wonder Woman?

Gunther looks baffled and less terrible.

'Cause she's a wonder?

Did you hear that? June says, carrying plates to the table. *That's pretty funny. Gunther's a funny guy, isn't he?*

I hope you like fish, June says to Leo. *I tried this teriyaki recipe I got from a friend, a millionaire actually, several times over.*

During dinner the kid is constantly pushing on his mother's mushy boundaries. She pleads with him and cajoles him and scolds him. Leo wonders what he's missing on TV.

The front door chimes, silencing them both, having a dreadful calming effect. June gets up to answer it. The boy listens to the oscillating tones coming from the hall, to the low voices over the background din of his heart beating.

Two civilians and a Mountie follow June into the living room. Gunther runs over to the couch and buries his face in the cushions.

Did you talk to Mel? June asks the one she knows.
No.

Why not? You're supposed to flag me. This is bull-shit.

We're obligated to investigate all complaints, says the one with the lime green hair.

Can we talk in the kitchen? June asks them, trying to spare Leo.

The workers acknowledge Leo with resigned smiles and follow June to the kitchen. The Mountie stands guard over dinner. Leo moves to the chair beside the sofa, to get a better view of the drama.

From the kitchen, muted voices carry tone but no distinguishable words. Gunther is so motionless on the sofa Leo understands that he's listening to them. When they return, June goes to her son.

We need to see your face, Gunther, she says, putting her hand on his back, gently shaking him. *Come on.*

But the boy won't budge and June's futile coaxing goes nowhere. She lifts him onto her lap but his hands stay glued to his face. Her attempts to pry them loose just get everyone frustrated. She leads the workers back to the kitchen.

Leo picks up the boy's doll. *Is this your doll, Gunther? Is this Wonder Woman?*

The boy's need to look overwhelms him, but he only looks long enough to nod that it is before his hands go back over his face and he buries his head in the cushions. Leo looks at the officer wondering if he saw anything from where he's standing, and the face shows something, or seems to. Leo can't be sure.

All three women are irritated and when June picks up the boy again there is more determination in her voice.

Please Gummy Bear. Do you know what you're doing to me?

Does he think he's helping her? Leo wonders. Whose interpretation of reality was he acting out? Perhaps hiding his father's authorship of all this, maybe stories he's heard of children being taken from their mothers in the middle of the night. Or was Gunther controlling his mother, abusing his power over her? There is a canny saneness about him.

June can't afford to let her emotions show and say something that might get added to her file. She needs to appear a certain way, to be a recognizable form, not the fragmented creature of their fabrications but one they can be comfortable with, one they won't feel the need to interpret. They were slashers with cookie-cutters and June hated them. They hated her too for making them feel ambiguous about their work.

How many times is this now?

It's been several, we know, but—

This is the fourteenth time. Don't you find it a little strange? Don't you think it means something when it's always the same person making the complaint?

The police officer speaks up: *I saw his face, he's fine.*

You sure? asks Lime Green, not sure she's willing to take his word.

Yah.

Okay then . . . says the senior worker, deadlock broken.

They leave and the room vibrates with their molecules.

Do you want me to heat it up? June asks.

No, it's even good cold. It's fine.

After they've eaten June makes coffee, which takes her half an hour in between finding lost toys and answering the boy's eager abuses with her aimless warnings. Leo smiles absently and glances at his watch while June carries on two conversations, one about the stock market that she thinks is for his benefit, and one about bedtime, which the boy is paying no attention to.

Two

LEO HATES DOCTOR'S waiting rooms. Sad cake holes slump on worried children. File folders multiply all over the walls behind the two receptionists. Shin-high tables are scabbed over with old magazines: *Yachting World, Money*. A morose Hindu woman leads him down a hall of doors. Behind the one she clips his file to he waits for another ten minutes. An ancient scale standing against the wall just for show seems to have outgrown its edges with all the layers of paint, the current one being blood red. The walls are framed with images of the human circulatory system and a diagram of a skinless man, and Leo wonders why life has to be so banal.

The doctor has a distracted sadness about him. Leo tells him about his problem urinating and goes into too much detail about his digestion issue, trying to be articulate about vague symptoms that may or may not be related: his depression, moods swings, the watery eyes, the undigested food in his stools. But the doctor is rubbing his chin and following his own thoughts, and when he gets the chance, steers the conversation back to what he apparently understands. He tells Leo to drop his pants as he pulls on a pair of rubber gloves. He encourages the flabbergasted Leo to bend over the table as he slathers a couple of fingers in jelly. Both men are tense, Leo thinking about the state of his underwear, the doctor working his fingers in, wiggling them to distribute the lubricant. Leo gasps when the doctor's persistent pressure pays off. The examination of his prostate takes a few seconds. In one movement the gloves come off with a snap and fly into a waste receptacle.

It's okay. It's enlarged, your prostate, but if it was cancerous it would be hard. Nothing too worrying.

Too worrying? Leo asks, feeling delicate.

You're middle-aged. It's not uncommon.

What about the other thing? Leo asks, feeling more close to the man, wanting to trust him.

The other thing? Oh, yes, the stools . . . well, it could be stress. I'll write you something for it.

Waiting for his prescription Leo wanders the aisles of the pharmacy, staring at pantyhose packaging and winking at the cosmetics consultant. Without his reading glasses all he can make out on the label of his medication is: *Don't operate motor vehicles or heavy machinery while taking this medication.* In the bakery next door he ponders the loaves on display, the aromas of wheat, and the suntanned cleavage of the woman waiting for him to decide between kaiser buns and a loaf of sourdough.

At home he makes a sandwich. It's been a week since his dinner with June and he's beginning to relax from the fright he got, from the stress of getting too close to a woman. He's reassured by his bachelor routines; no threat of double standards or kangaroo courts to loom on the horizon. From the fridge he gets a tomato and a chunk of mild cheddar. The mayonnaise jar, nearly empty, rings like a bell.

In the ragged back yard he moves a lawn chair into a patch of autumn sun. His places his tea on a Frisbee lying nearby and bites into his creation, discriminating the different textures, the tough crust, the yielding cheese, the cheerful cucumber, tomato with mayonnaise—together it all equalled a deep and lovely kiss. No wonder food and women were sometimes interchangeable. One of the things that impressed him about June was how well she cooked. The teriyaki salmon was right up there, thinking back on it, separating it out from everything else that night.

A cat steps into the yard to inspect objects on the uneven lawn, a laundry basket, a golf club. It peers from a coffee can and attacks a toy wheelbarrow. Leo tosses it a piece of cheese.

I wish you wouldn't feed them, June says, suddenly behind him.

Where's the harm in that? He twists around to look at her.

They pee in the garden.

He glances around for something you could call a garden but doesn't say anything.

They kill birds.

Yah, they do that; cats kill birds.

Why do they have to do that? She doesn't appreciate his tone.

They're jealous.

What are you talking about?

They wish they could fly?

Just don't feed them cheese; it's not good for them.

When they're eating my cheese they're not eating your birds.

They don't eat the birds, they torture them.

Gunther comes outside carrying a doll, which he drops in Leo's lap.

Ever play Cobbler, Gunther? Leo asks, taking one of the doll's shoes off and putting it on his finger. *This part's the upper, this is the shank.*

I need to run to the store, June says. *Can you keep an eye on him for a minute?*

Sure.

Gunther frowns as he watches his mother walk away down the alley.

Leo says, *Your doll has a hairline fracture of the first metatarsal.*

Gunther is too shy to respond.

There, we've added a first ray cut-out to her orthotics. You're a good father.

Leo is suddenly cold. He shifts his chair to where the sun has crept and Gunther goes for the cat.

With its wheels spinning and the extraction motor going the Sutton 1000 really howls. It has a wire rasp, a light sanding drum irreplaceably worn, and a belt with 24-grit sharks teeth, which Leo is hunched over, a work boot floating in his fingers in a manner that will allow the belt to capture the boot without taking his hands with it.

The running machine creates a thicket of sound, a good place to hide, and with his earplugs in he found it easy to daydream. He's being cared for by three homely but arousing nurses. They feed him thin soups and teach him about self-administered pain management. Lying on his deathbed he figures he's got enough time to leave his soul to science and have sex with the nurses a few more times.

Lee-o!

A voice like cars crashing breaks his reverie, unlocking the spring in his spine, propelling him away from the bloodthirsty wheels before he knows what's hit him. His muscles reel in the overdose of adrenaline, making him nauseous and angry. It's Marvin—inexperienced, dopey-eyed Marvin.

The fuck you do that for? Leo cries.

I'm standing here calling you.

This is Joe's progeny, his puss, the lanky body not quite filled out with man-flesh and body hair; the bemused face too easily deteriorates into a smirk.

Fucking idiot . . . Leo says.

Look, Marvin says, holding a shoe in Leo's face. A Nike, one Leo did last week. He kills power to the shaft but leaves the extractor going.

Look at the lift, Marvin says, straining over the noise.

And?

Two colours, both wrong. Joe nearly had a cow.

Joe wouldn't give a fuck about that.

Marvin cuffs the extractor switch and the men stare at one another while the impeller winds down.

Please, Marvin says, looking like he bit into an aspirin. *Can you just re-do it?*

Give it to me.

Correctly.

Marvin steps over the line. He doesn't know what he's done, but he isn't surprised when Leo takes his coat off the hook and leaves.

Under the bridge some jerk is inhaling fumes from a plastic bag. On the ground around him are killed glue tubes and empty nail polish bottles. When he sees Leo he mutters something innocuous which turns up the flame under Leo's mood.

What can I do for you? Leo says, taking a few steps towards him.

I don't want nothing. Leave me alone, the glue sniffer says, suddenly lucid.

He lopes away down the trail under the bridge, then stops and goes into the trees. Leo doesn't want to lose the intensity, following the man between blackberry streamers, footprints in the damp grass lead to a clearing where he is weaving like a reed in water. The sycamore leaves rattle under the ozone rain and traffic on the bridge rasps like someone dying. He can't sustain for somebody else what he reserves for himself. His self-hatred was a purer form, with its haughty disregard for everything he's worked for, his sobriety, his peace of mind.

A police cruiser in front of the house makes him double back through the alley. Inside he can hear the steeply pitched voice of June coming through the ceiling and the flatness of authority. Sitting on his unmade bed he manages to get only half undressed for his shower before lethargy shuts him down. He stares into a peripheral fog, listening to the drone of awful life. When the voices drive away, he drags himself to the kitchen and heats a can of soup.

He brings out a photo of his son he normally keeps

hidden in the back of a drawer. They say he was hand-some. A glint in his eye Leo used to think mischievous now seems spiteful. Benson was his mother's choice, the name. Leo would have called him David, as a tac-tile link to ancestors, a soldier uncle whose picture stood on Leo's mother's dresser, carried like code over the centuries, by men who were shaped by stone, who knew sacrifice, strong medicine. A name from a book severs something, weakens the immune system. Feelings are clawing at Leo's insides. He puts the pic-ture back in the drawer.

In bed no flutter of oblivion, no click of sleep. June is pacing above him. The boy wakes and she talks to him for a while, coaxing him back into his womb. But Leo is more awake than ever. The cogs and levers of existence make such a racket in his head. Insomnia is a dream about sleeping. The only time in his life he felt safe was after his son was born. The protective urges covered them both. To sleep with one ear open was to get the best sleep. How long now since Benson stepped off the chair? Except for the gesture of the body, the picture in Leo's mind always varies. Questions he should have asked at the time carry him further away from his own warmth. Solid details to pin down a men-tal picture. What was he wearing, was the bed made, how many paramedics did it take to cut him down? The image has a life of its own, except for the gesture, which is always the same. What did it mean, that deferential shrug, the opened palms? It should have been him, the ultimate act of a good father. What colour were his socks? What was the name of the motel?

He drinks a few handfuls of water to wash down one of the pills the doctor gave him. Leaning into the mirror, his hands grip the sides of the sink. There's a bottle of whisky in the cupboard. How did it get there? He remembers now. He bought it in case he had a guest. How casually he plots against himself. He imagines washing the rest of the pills down with a tumbler of whisky. Though all he was likely to get for his trouble was morning.

Someone is knocking on the adjoining door.

Hello? June's voice.

What are you doing here?

You got anything to drink?

He gets dressed, opens the bottle of whisky and pours her one.

That's six months down the drain, she says miserably.

They were here again, eh?

Can I have another?

He obliges.

And that's the next six months.

What did they say this time?

Were you in bed? Sorry. Mind if I take this? I'll pay you for it.

Take it.

You sure?

Marvin tells Leo there's someone in the store asking for him, the bird woman. He goes out front and she smiles a not altogether harmless smile, seeing through him right away, by his face. The geese could just as easily belong to a snake charmer at that moment, still as they are, appraising him too.

What can I do for you? he asks, stupidly.

Oh, you didn't remember.

Remember what? Going for complete ignorance.

We were counting on you.

For God's sake, he moans, giving too much away, *you should never count on me.*

She softens and says, *You have no faith.*

They're taking longer than I expected, he says.

Some people aren't capable of faith.

I'm looking forward to getting started. Now he feels an irresistible need to please.

You are, though, she says.

I'll have them ready for you in another week.

You have the beginnings of faith.

One week from today.

He opens the appointment book and glances at the clock on the wall.

And what was your name again?

Lasha, she tells him.

He puts her name in the book and in brackets puts "the bird woman."

One week from this exact heartbeat, he says.

She blushes.

He keeps leather scraps out of habit, his admiration for the material. Man's ridiculous genius hasn't come up with anything as durable and soft. He uncovers a nice piece of fine beige pigskin and compares it to the photocopy of the bird's feet. But he remembers, she doesn't like pigskin. He finds a lovely piece of alligator, but it's wrong somehow, for a goose. He digs up a couple of scraps of fine brown cow lining. He has no idea where to begin.

At home that night he tries sketching a few ideas on paper but he abandons the pencil's two-dimensional noise for a more productive folding and bending method, hoping a form, however nebulous, will start to take shape in the circuitry of his brain.

He hears a car pull up outside and he throws the leather down, giving up for now. June has visitors and tonight he's thankful he can't make out actual words.

Work is piling up, eight new orders coming in on Saturday, when the week ahead already exceeded his comfort level. When he's waiting for glue to dry or for Marvin to get off the grinder, he caresses the thin leather with his thumbs, turning it over in his mind and eventually the challenges coalesce into specifics and potential weaves itself into an idea, a place to begin.

Next day he nudges the creative process further along by abandoning needle and thread for a rivet gun. The course now reveals itself and he gets completely lost in the work.

Getting Marvin to help with production always backfires. He clutters up available surfaces with half-finished work and dominates the grinder where he accomplishes little. Leo takes the opportunity to put fasteners on the booties. He takes a stab at getting the finicky National to obey him. The sewing machine's take-up arm and tension disk must be in a precise mis-alignment, and for the thread to flow efficiently the bobbin must be wound by hand. The floor pedal has to be nursed into a nervous point between yes and maybe. The presser-foot lever needs to be continuously nudged with the wrist as he feeds material through.

Marvin is working on a boot whose sole he's ground away, which Leo is inspecting, eyeballing the contours, visualizing the bones, how their weight will bear. If Leo were doing it, he'd shave another two degrees of varus, but Marvin doesn't have that kind of skill. So Leo nods that it's fine and hands it back to him, and Marvin rubs his neck and stares at the work order. It always defies stock solutions, orthopaedic work. Everything Leo knows he has pretty much extrapolated from the spaces between what they tell him. The science is convoluted and little of it trickles this far. Regardless how detailed, the work orders inevitably missed the focal point. Intuition is nearly always required; but how reliable is it with shoes? Joe and Marvin espouse conflicting definitions of basic concepts, which they debate but never resolve.

When the bird woman comes back Leo is ready. He puts a pair of poorly conceived leather things on the counter before her.

They are exquisite, she says, delighted.

They're okay.

They are more than exquisite.

Definitely adequate. Leo knows they are a poor piece of work.

Now getting them on . . .

Leo anticipated this in the design. He opens them out flat on the counter and she encourages Little One to step right into them. Then he folds the flaps up, snug but not too tight.

Even fasteners!

Velcro, he says proudly.

I don't know how I'm going to repay you, aside from what you're going to charge.

You've already done that.

How much does the bill come to?

The amount of labour that goes into hand-crafting a pair of shoes tends to make the cost prohibitive.

A craftsman has to earn a living.

I'm no craftsman.

But what can I do for you?

Leo is feeling large, contented. He looks at Marvin over by the cash register.

Just pray for my soul, he says.

You have a beautiful soul.

You have no idea.

Marvin holds the door open, where she pauses to look back at Leo with a calm sadness. Leo feels awkward after the encounter and he goes back to the Sutton to hide in his work.

The next day a headache shadows him to work; a blind-spot drifts across his field of vision, and he decides to be late for work and sits down on one of the benches beside False Creek. Another day's inexplicable weather. He watches boats go by. The jagged void in his vision gradually disappears off the edge of the city.

When the trail takes him under the bridge, the sun has just risen over the roofs, and at that moment the viscous gold light catches thousands of glass fragments in the shanty soil.

The headache is with him all morning and his work doesn't flow. He's in too much of a hurry and not getting enough done. His thoughts inflict on him their futile rehearsals of doom and conversations he will never have. He slips with the knife and the blade slices through the heel of his hand. His meat is brown and pink. The gash fills with blood and spills like oil. He tracks blood to the bathroom and smears the emergency kit looking for a compress. The cut is deep and long, serious enough for stitches, but he's dealt with worse. Every knuckle is tagged and every finger eviscerated in one way or another: from the diverse jobs and hungers, the years break and accumulate, zigzag, set badly. Injury structures memory; it's a gradual process of naming. He wraps it up tight in gauze and goes back to work.

After lunch Joe calls him into his office. A remnant of a sandwich clings to the man's white moustache. On the bookshelf a chipped Buddha grins furiously with a cigar stuck in its mouth.

Wan' a java, Leo?

No thanks, Joe.

No? You sure? I do, damn it, he says, getting up on his short legs, grabbing his cup.

The desk is covered with papers, most pockmarked with coffee stains, and a jar of pens—most of them out of ink, which Joe chucks back in the jar when they don't work, grabbing another, eventually hitting on one with ink—and a picture of his daughter taken at least ten years earlier, and one of Marvin in kindergarten. Joe returns, slopping coffee. He leans back in his chair and knits his fingers behind his head, bumping a picture of the Manchester United soccer club.

Leo, Leo, Leo . . . he says, shaking his white head.

Their relationship has always been based on honesty. Leo can look him in the eye and tell him he's full of it. It's something Joe values about Leo. Since Leo's trouble, however, they have talked less.

So, how's the coffee today, Joe? Leo asks.

Same as always.

Like crap, you mean.

If you like.

Maybe I will get a cup.

I insist.

Leo hunts up a mouldy mug, washing it in the bathroom sink.

Joe is wearing a pained look when he returns.

You okay? Leo asks.

Don't I look okay?

Not really.

I wonder if I'm coming down with something.

There's a flu going round.

Oh yah? Chicken or pig?

A hybrid apparently. Seems they've made a chicken out of a pig, or some such thing.

It's genetic tampering. What do they think is going to happen?

They can't decide whether to call it a picken or a chig.

Joe looks at him over his glasses. Leo doesn't know why he screws with the man's head. He tries to start the conversation over.

What can I do for you, Joe?

Unsure of where to begin, Joe says, *It happened again this morning . . .*

What happened again?

Coming in late.

What do you mean late? Leo is surprised.

What part of late do you not understand?

You're forgetting our agreement.

What agreement?

My flexible hours. We have an understanding.

With Marvin?

With you.

And we actually had a conversation about it?

It was a gentleman's agreement.

We're not playing on the same soccer field, my friend.

It's not a soccer game, for Pete's sake. Leo is getting defensive.

Joe chooses his words with care, *In a way it is a soccer game, Leo. One where everyone is allowed a certain number of errors.*

What errors?

Working on a "left" when the work order says "right," a "right" when it says "left," wrong colour. Casualties of you being so . . .

It's been a bad year.

For all of us, Leo. For all of us.

Leo doesn't know what he means by that but it makes him angry, his selfish refusal to see Leo's tragedy as anything other than a problem for himself.

It's the customer comes out the loser, Joe says, taking a slurp of his coffee.

The customer should win?

There you go.

So it's inevitable that we have to lose?

Never mind the freakin' soccer game. Jesus H. Christ, man . . . how do you do that?

I'm just trying to understand.

And my arse is the king of France.

I don't understand what the king of France has to do with your ass, Joe.

You used company materials, on company time, to make that woman shoes for her . . . bird, and you didn't charge her a red cent.

What, that nice harmless old woman? What have you got against her?

It's like you're trying to drag everybody down a hole with you.

Leo doesn't understand. Is he missing something? Did he walk in on somebody else's conversation?

You have to make everything so complicated. Fuck Leo, I thought we were friends.

I'm fired?
I'm sorry to be so blunt.

Leo walks north on Granville Street, oblivious to the emaciated Peter Pans in the one-way doors, through downtown's conflux of mirrors, turning west on Georgia and down through the Bayshore lot into the park. How many times has he walked the seawall in the decade since he arrived here with nothing in his sack but urges? It was a nipple of heaven, with downtown reflecting in the harbour like a diamond necklace. He wed her that night, the city, burned her desperate rain into his circuits, her avaricious gloom. Why don't people ever get used to it, to loss? There is so much of it, whole entire cities. His father worked hard to put loss on the table, loss of self-respect, loss of safety, loss of the knowledge of pleasure. The only constant then was moving, until it was the most valuable commodity in the world, what you took to the bank, what you draped over the dead.

When Leo is halfway around the park he looks up to see the elderly bridge, all grand in her pearl bridal veil, holding her skirt up out of the water where she wades. He climbs up through the forest on the service road until he's on the overpass looking down onto the deck, where instinct for survival was the only thing keeping the cars apart. He walks out on the uneven sidewalk, imagining for a second the drop, tasting its vertigo when he stares down at the narrows' cold chop, wondering what it took, cowardice or guts. Every city had its own language of death, its whorish old monuments. Vancouver has bridges, articulating over the years a word for sincerity, for the chink in that which was intended, where the real marrow could be tasted. To accept about yourself that which you could never accept. Loss, he should be used to it, memorable failures, the back-firing wife, and then his mother was gone too, consolidating all the losses into one final payment.

They were together for eight years before Julie walked out and took Benny with her back east. They were in Calgary at the time, their last attempt at having a somewhere. Leo was happy, too, with the novelty of clockwork rain and the depth of the sky over the Great Plains, and the foothills like storybooks laying open, with their pop-up fences and paper horses. Until he stopped being happy, that is, until it got to him, the jagged west, the unrequited coital whiff he swore sometimes wafted over from the sea.

He drove them to the airport and walked as far as the metal detector, where they spent their last moments as a family. She went through without a qualm or a blip, but Benson stopped, wide-eyed with self-doubt, up against tearing himself in two. His mother was beckoning him to be brave, Leo telling him it was going to be okay. And when he courageously stepped through, he set off the alarms. A cloudburst could not have been more desolate. The trouble was caused by Leo's parting gift, the keyring that was to include a truck when the boy turned sixteen. It was a valuable lie, which they both understood, a way to say good-bye and not say good-bye. But Julie summarily tossed it into a repository for bad ideas and strode away, the towed boy looking back at his brand new past.

Walking home from the park, Leo caught reflections of himself in store windows, not recognizing himself, so detached and dignified he seemed, like an old hand, a proud, strong alloy. Night settled over the city like a lizard on her eggs and he walked beside the evening ribbon of traffic, as though for some reason our last moments were best spent in a car. Standing on the traffic-wild Burrard Bridge, three-quarters blind and nine-tenths asleep, he stared down at the water of False Creek, and all the lights that burned on its shore.

Sweaty and tired when he gets home, he stands in his bathroom, unwrapping the pointless bandage on his hand. He should have got stitches. The cut blossoms like a rose, like his inside trying to get out. He washes it with hydrogen peroxide and gets most of the dried blood off. As he opens the medicine cabinet for a bandage, the lights go out. He's aware of the smell of steam and an overheated coil; the kettle, he'd plugged it in when he got home. The clinging darkness is noisy with residual light. He hears a knocking and June's voice.

Leo?

I'm here.

Did you blow a fuse?

Probably a breaker.

Do you know where the box is?

No.

A small flame appears on her thumb, reflected in her star sapphire eyes. The scent she's wearing has a stormy wildness about it, and he longs for the sheltering nape of being in love, to be out of reach of his memories. He wants to get on his knees and beg her to love him. But the glare of banality breaks over them when June locates the switch.

The empty kettle starts hissing again and Leo yanks the plug from the socket. He cracks the seal on a new bottle of whisky and offers her a drink.

I walked around Stanley Park tonight, he tells her.

Why?

There needs to be a why? he asks, realizing he doesn't want to talk about it.

Of course, tell me, she says, dropping onto the couch and putting her drink on the floor.

He sits on the other end and she stretches a leg over his knees. He takes her shoe off and examines the wear patterns and smells it.

Don't do that, she cries, gently kicking.

You can tell a lot about a person.

Like what?

Trade secret.

The sole was mute with unexploited life lines, a strange mortal frailty about feet, translucent and pale.

Tell me.

Let's see, he says, sampling the shoe again. Women aren't one hundred percent animal. Their feet don't smell in the same affronting way. They are creatures of habit, not gravity.

I can tell that you like lime Jell-O, he says.

They make that stuff from horses. Did you know that?

You have nightmares about being alone and you're a free spirit. He tries to hypnotize her with contradictions.

What did you do to your hand? she yells, pushing him away. *That is too gross. Yuk. Did you have to let me see that? I'm sorry, but I'm going.*

Take the bottle, he says, going to finish cleaning and dressing his wound.

Can I?

He sits at the table and gets lost in a memory of his son, the time they rented a cabin up the coast. Benson was starting university that fall. He was joining the ranks of daydreamers and soft men. Their little cabin was on the rocky shore. It was littered with kelp and washing up one morning came a dead sheep. Where was its starting point, to arrive at this specific and random beach? Leo wanted to know. He pestered his son with metaphysical claptrap and drank too much. The smelts were running and gulls overran the place with their subterfuge. Most of the time they sat in separate corners and read.

The eternal bottleneck of unemployment, he doesn't know why it has to feel as it does with its keepsake burdens of guilt and blame. He has always contributed to the ungrateful machine, put in his wasted hours, taken his portions of pride as payment.

To dislodge himself from the oppressive room he closes his eyes, though he can't escape the awful humming in the ceiling and the close factual air. He looks around for something to read, finding tracts on teenage pregnancy, on avoiding disease, all written to discourage life, regurgitating the old wives' tale that the world doesn't owe you a living—remanufacturing the truth into a system of loopholes—when everybody knows that it does. He steps up to the counter and starts to tell the woman that he wants to apply for unemployment, and she tells him to go through the door on the right, into another waiting area.

He ransacks the paper every afternoon and makes calls first thing in the morning. He wants to stay away from the shoe trade; the little shops never pay that much. He wants a real job, with a pension plan and extended medical, the kind they retire you from with a watch. He reaches into past lives for skills long dormant, visualizes himself in positions filled by much younger men. Employment Insurance turned him down for benefits, because of the way he was fired, having brought it on himself. But that was fine with him because he was determined to find something else. But pounding the pavement and beating the bushes for a month has got him nowhere but here, scouring the classified section, looking for a cheaper place to live.

In Apartments for Rent, there's nothing for under $685 a month. In Rooms to Rent he finds nothing under four hundred. In Shared Accommodation, he circles one for $275. He can imagine the place, loners and schizophrenics, though it has a west side location going for it. Finding his phone dead reminds him of other bills he hasn't paid.

June is talking on the phone when he knocks, promoting one of her penny stocks. Leo goes up and waits for her to finish the call, drumming the rolled up classified on his knee.

He starts aimlessly snapping Lego pieces together.

What are you making? Gunther asks.

Don't know yet.

Is it a house?

Maybe.

June's lipstick is fresh and dark when she returns.

You're good with him, she says.

Can I use your phone?

What is it? asks the boy, of what Leo has made.

Can't you tell? He hands it to him.

See what Leo made?

I have to move.

Oh no.

Can I use your phone?

How much are you paying for rent down there?

More than I can handle.

Way less than I pay up here though.

Leo picks up the receiver and dials the number listed in the paper.

It's a big old house in Shaughnessy, a firetrap. The lilac bushes and linden trees seem to hold the potential for despair. The neighbours must hate the place. Standing on the porch he detects the scent of incense. He spins a thickly painted and chipped handle that connects to a bell on the other side of the door. Through wavy glass he can make out the shape of a woman coming down the hall.

I've come about the room? Leo says.

Look who has come to take the room, speaking to the geese at her feet. *I was praying to the goddess Sita.*

Alarmed, he steps in. Battered hardwood floors, scarves hiding flaws in the sofa, and a big embracing chair that lords it over the room. An exploded piece of sheet metal hangs on a wall. And the room smells faintly avian.

The bird woman is wearing a pink rayon evening gown and a straw sun hat. The stroller is standing in the hall.

Come, she says, *I will show you around,* steering him into the kitchen.

We share the cooking. There are normally six of us, so we each take one night a week. Saturdays we fend for ourselves. Same with breakfasts and lunch. We have a community pot for basics like rice, potatoes, pasta. Here we keep track of extra things, luxuries.

A list on the inside of the cupboard door has names and dollar amounts beside unpromising items like caraway seeds and rice cakes. At the table a man with a long grey ponytail is reading. *This is Narayan,* she says.

How's it going? I'm Leo, he says, taking the man's large hand, his smile which seems to mock.

Following her down the hall he's thinking he could never live here. She and her birds he could handle, he can always get along with women. It's other men.

She leads him up a creaking staircase while he hangs back to get a better look at her. Her legs might be too short but he isn't sure. It could be the dress, an optical illusion. In the upper hall, a lamp with mushy light and a musty thickness in the air. A cracked washbasin standing on a side table, dried flowers in a vase.

That's the great thing about dried flowers, Leo says, *they don't need much watering.*

One room is in the basement, she says, *three rooms on the main floor, and just two up here.*

She opens a door and lets him in while she stays in the hall. Will his things even fit? After all his purges? Probably. Holding the curtain aside he likes the neighbour's clean-shaven yard.

The other man on this floor is an artist, she tells him. *He's a private person too,* she says, revealing that she has been observing him.

Does he work in acrylics or oils?

Dynamite, she says.

It's $275? he asks.

You don't smoke?

The geese, where do they live?

In my room, of course.

What about the other tenants?

Daniel and Josephine. She's a student; he's a cyclist.

Another man to make him anxious. He wonders what this Josephine is going to look like.

I guess I'll take it, he says.

Three

L EO OPENS THE upstairs bathroom window as wide
as it goes and pulls the door closed behind him.
His work boots echo on the stairs. Condiment bottles
in the fridge door jingle and he pours a glass of juice.
He drops bread into the toaster. Everything at six A.M.
is noisy: the rasp of a knife on toast, the lonely tapping
of spoon against cereal bowl. Lasha's room is next to
the kitchen and her door is open for the convenience
of the birds. Leo can hear her whispering in her sleep.

He walks as quietly as possible down the hall, past
Daniel's room and Josephine's, then steps onto the
porch and closes the heavy door like a thief. He
makes the thirty-minute walk to his new job at
Canplas with enough time to sit on the toilet before
his shift starts.

Heading out on the floor he nods to the man he
takes over from, slipping gloves on, adjusting the

rubber mat where he's to spend the next eight hours. Giving no quarter-hour for shift changes, the injection mold gapes open and forces Leo into the breech. He lifts the newly minted PVC pipe fitting off the pressure face and hinges it on a steel peg at waist level. He inserts the second positive and it closes to gestate another black joint. Returning his attention to the one on the bench he removes the inside form and tosses the three-inch Y into an overflowing bin. Leo reassembles the positive form, ready for the next cycle, and has a twenty-two-second wait where he reads half a page of a Doc Savage novel, something he found in the lunch room. The machine gapes open, demanding Leo move quickly through the process again, lifting it out, replacing the second inside form, removing the fitting, checking for flaws, assembling the first form, then reading the same half page of Doc Savage, trying to find the place where he left off.

On Friday the foreman is standing beside the time clock handing out paycheques. He tells Leo he wants him on nights next week. Leo is appalled by night shifts, how it screws with his internal clock, how it swallows up the only thing he has left, his evenings for long walks.

He looks at the man, at the large pores on his small nose, the stupid look in his eyes.

I'd rather not, he says.

You have to. Everyone does.

I really can't. I was hoping there was some way we could figure this out.

There isn't.

There must be something.

I'm not going to stand here and argue about it with you, the foreman says, getting edgy.

I didn't know we were arguing.

Don't piss in my ear . . .

Fuck you.

You want a taste of this? The foreman squeezes a fist.

Leo drops his apron at the man's feet. *Just try it,* he says, leaning in close to the foreman's face, *you fat fucking ignorant inbred piece of shit.*

When he gets home Lasha is on the living room floor with her birds. The stroller is turned over and she's holding a screwdriver. Leo takes the sofa and smiles at Josephine who looks up for a second from her laptop. A determined look on Lasha's face gives away that she has no idea what she's doing. He wonders how her mind works, how she can survive in a technical world without the ability to connect details to their receptor details. He gets down on the floor with her.

Want me to have a look?

Please. I'm lost.

I can see that.

The geese insert their scary heads into the spaces

around them and Leo holds his elbows up for protection.

Have you ever oiled the wheels? he asks.

Oil?

Do you have any?

Cooking oil.

Any Three-in-One, or WD40?

I don't think so.

Daniel would have something, Josephine says, half coming out of her screen.

Leo doesn't want to ask Daniel. He doesn't like him, his sad eyes and vague hands, and the way he keeps to himself, always cleaning his pride and joy two-thousand-dollar racing bike.

What about Stephen? Is he home? asks Lasha.

Stephen, the dynamite artist, the only one in Canada, according to a piece the *Province* did on him. Deep life is carved in his face and his yellow-grey hair has a permanent slept-on look. Faint chemical odours come from his room and from off his person sometimes, but he swears that he keeps no explosives in the house. Aside from his chrome-plated explosion on the wall there are more pieces in the basement.

How about you? Leo asks Josephine. *Do you have any oil?*

I do, actually, she says, amazed at herself for not remembering.

She doesn't return immediately so Leo goes over

and leans on the frame of her door, looking at her unmade bed and the stacks of papers and the piles of
books, and her, haphazardly searching drawers and
cupboards.

Her dissertation is a mouthful, titled *Features of
Event Horizon Geography.* In it she theorizes that
time actually goes backwards, that it's not a linear
phenomenon at all, a contraction rather than a contradiction. What he finds most interesting about it
though is the way her bum sticks out when she tries
explaining it to him.

I can't find it, she says, meaning the oil.

You sure? He steps over the threshold of her room
to help her look.

It was here. I thought I saw it fairly recently, she
tells him.

On her face is usually a distracted expression, but
once in a while she comes out from behind it, which
he finds she is doing now, studying him.

It's right there, he says, flustered by her complicated body language, his gaze falling on a can of WD40 on
the window ledge beside a shrunken orange.

Oh, there it is, she says, amused with herself, and dis-
gusted, pleased that Leo is in her room and unhappy
that she doesn't know what to do about it.

Leo sprays the stroller's wheels, spins them a few
times, and turning it over gives it a hopeful push on
the rug. One wheel shudders a little.

There you go, he says to Lasha, *good as new.*

Clean Steel is a misnomer. Scrap metal cannot be clean. It's in the process of turning to dust. Leo can feel the gritty decay through the holes in his gloves, wearing out a pair a day, moving chunks of steel from one pile to another. When Stephen told him they needed another man, he immediately got on the phone to the owner. Determined to make it work, he was impressive for the first few days, and it wasn't easy, scrabbling about beneath three pyramids of scrap metal and dodging the sociopath working the crane.

He takes a coffee break next to the slow and resolute river on a little patch of sand he found between a ship's anchor and a crushed car, grateful to be motionless and half asleep, to feel the breeze.

Driving home after work Stephen tells Leo that machines have an afterlife in his art. He tells him about the objects he finds, broken machines and parts dislodged from the firmament of usefulness. The resurrected souls of things ride home with them in the back of his pickup.

At Clean Steel, Leo is asked to man a machine they call The Beast. Switch it on and one giant arm moves down over the other, patiently, untiringly. Wanting only to be hand-fed, it slices inch-thick steel like paper. With no guard around the giant pincher, and the emergency off-switch located such that it would only be useful as an afterthought, Leo is reluctant to begin. He stands there watching it go, scratching his head, imagining the worst. When he does select a piece of steel, a long one, so he can stand back, he feels a seductive pull and release, the metal twisting, then yielding like cartilage.

The men watch as Leo and the owner walk across the yard. Idly following, the men gather around The Beast and listen to Leo's speech about loose bootlaces, decapitations and bad luck. They nod and make respectful sounds. The owner listens to Leo's ideas about building a guardrail and relocating the kill-switch. He nods his apparent agreement when Leo points out the numerous hazards. He reassigns Leo to paint the shed then turns around and assigns someone else to The Beast.

One hot August day a DC9 Caterpillar tractor arrives on a semi-trailer. The driver hangs from his door as the men gather round. Stephen climbs all over it, running his hands over the fat yellow body, feeling for something distant and cool. They can find no markings to indicate its weight and there's nothing on the waybill that isn't smudged and illegible. Their guesses range between twenty and fifty tons.

The crane operator sidles over, a playfulness in him Leo has never seen before. Squinting through cigarette smoke, he says he can lift it off with the crane, winking at Leo. He goes to manoeuvre the crane over.

Detaching the magnet he shows them where to run the cables under the Cat and how to loop them into the crane's grapple. He jumps into his careworn seat and lights a cigarette off the one that's nearly done. His awkward body is nimble in the cab of his crane as he throws handles, nurses clutch levers, pumps the foot pedals. Black smoke pours from the exhaust as he guns it meditatively, enticing slack from the cable. Testing the opposing forces, tentatively embracing them, he makes the tracks of the crane dance in the silky dust and the bed of the semi undulate like water. He leans into the hydraulics and nearly stalls the engine. Ignoring the shouts for him to stop, he throws everything he's got into it, and the boom twists and crashes down into the group of scrambling men.

The owner comes charging out of his trailer, begging to hear that no one was hurt, demanding to know what happened. The men all stand there with nothing to say, wiping foreheads with sleeves, or awkwardly scratching their nuts.

Fuming mad, he turns to Leo.

Tell me what happened, he demands.

Why are you suddenly interested in my opinion? Leo asks.

I'm not. You're fired! he screams.

The crane operator lights up a cigarette and winks at Leo.

Since June stopped working, there is time to be a mother again, if that isn't a contradiction. Time is Gunther and motherhood is geography. He clings to her like moss, like his own personal slab. Rick shows up to work his claim and the ministry keeps records on her moods. Her own mother, an ocean away, wants landscape architects and surveyors to wrap her in the Union Jack.

Cabbage soups, canned fish casseroles; fresh veggies, yes, but fresh fruit, no, too expensive; between Gunther and his playmates they can go through a whole bowl in a day. Having given up cable, the only channels they get are fuzzy locals, one of which Gunther is staring at, not fully engaged in the adult cartoon that's on. Maybe he's working out a solution to the world's problems. Maybe he's thinking about his dad.

Rick has him on weekends and insists he wants more time, but if things are going bad with Gunther, or good in his personal life, then he doesn't want him at all. He pays no support when he's not working, and when he's flush he finds lavish ways to spend money on the boy or he brings out his list of excuses. It's difficult for June, the constant struggle to fend off his fictions, particularly the ones about how she screwed up his life. She doesn't know where the guilty feelings come from. His life has always been what it is now. At the moment he's selling flooring, which June has trouble comprehending. Rick in sales. He's unpredictable and edgy on all but his very best days.

She's reluctant to challenge him, but she will on occasion, like she did this morning, when he showed up to borrow twenty dollars. Her patience was all used up by ten in the morning, and when he insisted, she blew up at him, called him a loser and a hypocrite. She only wanted him to look at himself but it came out as an attack. He was wounded and had to make a big deal about his delicate pride.

She fries ground turkey, boils potatoes, just the way Gun' likes them. But when she puts it in front of him he refuses to eat. They fall into the familiar pattern of her trying to be reasonable and him cranking up the chaos. Before long she has resorted to making him feel guilty and he laps it up.

While she does the dishes he careens around above her head with the children of the new upstairs tenants. When June decided to move into Leo's old space, the cheaper basement suite, she had no idea it was going to be so noisy. She pays half the rent and gets twice the noise. Their blood-curdling play ricochets off the walls, with heads being lopped off and bodies hacked to bits, until Kate, the twins' mother, at the end of her tether, with the shriek to end all shrieks, shuts them up for a while.

Just as often June has the whole crew in her place

where they have considerably less room. She organizes painting parties that go wrong, disastrous cookie bakes, and shoots them dead with the smoking finger, or collapses into a heap when it's her turn to be it, just grateful for the one hundred seconds of peace.

Later they watch half an hour of fuzzy TV. June pours the last drink from a bottle she's had sitting there for weeks, wondering who she can call, later, when her son settles down, when she starts to get lonely. She turns her book to the page with Leo's new number and puts it beside the phone.

There's a knock at the door and she gets up to answer it. Three social workers are standing there looking vulnerable in the glare of the bare bulb. In any other context they might be somebody's friends come to call. It's Lime Green, though her hair is a spacey red colour now, and the other two, a man and a woman, June has never seen before.

Can we come in? Lime Green asks.

Her face conveys an assertion of power and deference in an attempt to communicate that their being here isn't necessarily a bad thing. On the one hand is concern for doing their job, which isn't necessarily the same as doing the right thing. On the other hand is her concern for June, but not for what she might be going through, or how unfair this all might be, but rather that she not make the wrong move and be brought down by the system.

No, she says, lobbing the door closed in their collective face and hitting the lock.

She goes to Gunther and picks him up. Together they listen to the obstinate knocking and are both startled by the sound of the door giving way to force. Gunther struggles from her grip and runs into the bedroom. June blocks them in the hall. Lime Green speaks: *We understand how difficult this is.*

You don't understand anything.

Can we see Gunther? asks the new woman.

He's afraid of you.

Where is he?

Leave us alone.

What are you trying to hide? Lime Green again. June is bewildered, incapable of fighting a tactic like that. They get past her into the living room.

She regroups before the bedroom door.

Why are you doing this? June asks.

We received a complaint.

You know who it was from.

We are obliged to . . .

You must be so stupid, June can think of nothing else to say.

I see no reason to get personal, says the woman.

You're clowns, evil fucking clowns.

We had a report that you were manic.

Can't you see we're having a pleasant evening here?

If that's true, where's the boy?

More baffling logic.

Fuck you. Just go fuck yourself!

They seem momentarily unsure of their ground. Lime Green dials her cell phone and walks around the apartment, prying beneath sheets of paper, pushing cigarette butts around an ashtray, searching for evidence of life on Mars. In the kitchen she studies the empty whisky bottle; and the whole time talking in a low voice to her hand.

We have to look at him, says the male to June.

He doesn't want you looking at him.

We have to do our job.

Why do you have to do your job?

Why do you make this so difficult?

The woman has read June's file. There's that word, "difficult."

A police car pulls up outside and two officers meet Lime Green on the lawn. The officers come in and start going through drawers and cupboards in the kitchen, and while June is distracted by this the workers get into the bedroom to examine Gunther.

It's clearly Lime Green's element, suspended there between alternatives, tough choices, struggling with different agendas: hers, the ministry's, trying to see the angles, how they justify, measure up against her bias or her grudges. June watches the competing thoughts line up on her face, as conclusion overthrows conclusion.

She looks up into June's terrified face and, seeing the vulnerability there, mistakes it for hatred. Frustrated, she opts to exercise her power.

Okay, I've decided, she says, looking past June, *we're taking the child.*

What? You can't do that, June bawls.

Gunther is reaching for his mother, trying to say something through the thick anaesthesia of his terror, as the women carry him out. The two cops are getting ready to call it a night, standing there in the deafening silence. Lime Green turns to say something to June, some bureaucratic wisdom, but June will hear no more shit from this childless cunt. She grabs a handful of her red hair and slings her into a beam, and drops her like a sack of dung.

June is inarticulately drowning. Her life was merely a bad dream but she's in hell now. The speed of her heart pounding, the ambulance churning through the streets. A paramedic is heroically saving one of the ministry's fallen soldiers while June is pressed into agony by a cop kneeling on her legs, squeezing her face into the floor. When someone crams a lit hypo into her ass, her hell becomes a fuzzy hell. Trying to swim up to the surface, she twists in the undertow and vomits. The siren suddenly stops wailing and they move down two corridors at once, the social worker down one pastel hallway lined with her colleagues, while June is deposited in a room with the same cop, deemed to be in need of some restraint.

You're hurting me, June mutters in her haze. *Why are you doing this?*

Because I can?

Have you got children you bastard?

Stillness is all the answer she needs.

You better keep an eye on them, she hisses.

The bookshelf in the living room has a Romanian translation of Shakespeare and a book about sex addiction. The rest of them belonged to Narayan, his six translations of the Bhagavad-Gita, several Bibles, books on yoga, biographies of Hitler and Ghandi, and in the basement more boxes of his religious books, dating back through his phases, starting with university days up to his present disillusionment. He spent six months in India and discovered a deep rooted pettiness in its people. Criticized for entering a temple in jeans, he rebuffed his critic with a lecture about peasant dress, and cultural equivalents. He doesn't like when people make it too easy for him to feel superior. A picture of the yogi who gave him his Hindu name sits on the top shelf.

Leo leans the portrait of his son against a vase on the middle shelf. He wants to reclaim the image.

Only a likeness after all, thin as a coat of paint, less substantial than memory. But he sees himself in the boy's smile, and the promise having a son meant for him, for Leo, giving him the drive to prosper, the dull parent following clear-eyed youth. But he wonders now did it work that way? How'd we get to this eternal candy store, to a culture of self-gratification and mommy?

Who is that a picture of? Lasha asks.

My son.

How old is he?

He would be twenty.

Oh.

He's ready to spill his guts but her eyes glaze over. She won't let him explore her with his problems.

He died young, Leo persists.

She looks at him for a few seconds and asks if he wants to go to the store. Thinking it an invitation to talk, he goes to his room for his jacket and waits for her on the porch. But she reappears as the bird woman and starts preparing the stroller for the trip.

You don't want to come?

Don't hate me.

My dear man . . . she says smiling.

He lies on his bed and as soon as he closes his eyes the image of his son snaps, swaying with leftover momentum, above the ever-widening question of why. All the details of his life were tidy. His bills were paid.

There was no note, no reason, no sentimental claptrap to cover over the shocking, appalling anger. Nothing. Leo retraces in his mind his steps that day, trying to recall the places he went, to remember his moods, sifting for a premonition, anything. It was a workday, an average day. He was exhausted after work. Was there a feeling, a fragment of an inkling of one? All he gets is the gesture of a hanged man. Was it a shrug, a gag?

The funeral was a display of getting on with it, calm and lucid, the most inhuman he'd ever seen Julie's parents. At a loss for how to grieve, they stood together, setting aside legitimate grievances for this one true meaning, consummated in its loss. Alone we are offered, alone can we perceive that in the end all is brutality, be it a quick thud or the slow slide, the collapse of parted seas.

The phone in the hallway keeps ringing and Leo ignores it until it stops. But now he wonders who it was. When it starts ringing again he hurries downstairs to get it.

Hello, he moans.

Leo, it's me.

What's wrong?

The wheel of the stroller. The girls are frightened.

The wheel came right off?

Yes. I think so. It's leaning.

Where are you?

The market.

I'll be right there.

He straps on his tool belt and heads out the door, miserable and groggy, obsessed with the need to relieve her distress as quickly as possible. He ignored the obvious problem with the wheel. The tools swinging on his belt oscillate and don't permit him to hurry. Why does he bring a hammer, a tape measure? He doesn't know. That's just it. She deserves better.

When he gets there, Lasha is chatting amiably with a child. Little One is demure in her leather booties and Ophelia has decided to walk in the road. It irritates Leo that he knows them so well. A man should not be required to have relationships with fowl.

Kneeling to see what can be done with the stroller he finds the axle broken. Lasha nods while he explains the problem, then he goes into the store to spend his last five dollars on a roll of duct tape. He walks home with them, to keep an eye on his repair job, and though he tries to conceal it, he feels ashamed to be walking beside the bird woman; it's her brazen showiness, the curiosity she makes of herself. But with his tool belt he supposes he completes the picture. But watching how people react to her he realizes something: the joy in their faces had not a trace of scorn. That Lasha was really a very shy person had eluded him, and that it wasn't easy for her, this performance; it wasn't a frivolous thing.

Four

LEO DREAMS OF finding a quiet lover, a woman in possession of herself, not him. Stillness was a feature to be ranked with perfect breasts and a sundress silhouette. He wanted a woman's thoughts to read, to investigate them with discreet observations, to join the threads of her life and make sense of her dreams. She would be like a stone on a hillside that hadn't moved in eons, but was still capable of flight.

Most women he's known cast every thought in words. They boast of negligible victories and rant importantly over trivia. They expect you to rewrite history to line up with their kitchen wallpaper. Kidding around with Benson's mother was like teasing a chair. How can you live without irony? How can you have irony without silence? It was a relief when the baby came along and she had someone else to dazzle with her succinct gibberish. Since then with lovers it's been the same sad sideshow. As though words had substance beyond that of a spider's abandoned radar dish.

But then there's Josephine walking beside him, who hasn't spoken for at least ten minutes. She walks swiftly, her hands in her pockets, head down. After a brief stab at small talk when they started out at daybreak, the nervous tension eased. She has a bubble of her own, he's noticed, that she slips in and out of. But Josephine could never be his lover, too eccentric and too young. Without a word she steers him through the uncharming streets of Marpole, just an adept nudge from her pointy shoulder. He would find this irritating if he weren't so pacified by its directness.

What might have been lovely about the neighbourhood is lined with factories and docks and spanned by concrete bridges. Freighters finesse the winding channel to unload Japanese cars in Delta, to steal away with lumber from mills in New West. Miles of riverbank reinforced against the relentless wake with boulders from distant quarries and concrete from deconstruction and collapse. At four in the morning the city is simply grotesque and rises like an amphitheatre above the levee where the din of industry goes on without end, with the clang of hammer on tank, the rhythmic cascade of raw materials.

They come to an ordinary garage off a residential alley in a nondescript part of the neighbourhood. It's an imperfect intersection of a handful of paper routes, a busy point on the early morning landscape of dark bedrooms. An unobtrusive young guy manages the district from the seat of his dull red Fiat. A former paperboy, one of the last of his breed, a refugee from the domain of premature days and black winter wind. Familiar territory for Josephine, as well, who was drafted by an older brother and being the youngest sibling had no successor. Delivery boys now were mostly retired gentlemen and unskilled mothers with hatchbacks. They pushed at the boundaries only to be outrun by the poverty line. The odd purist still existed, pulling away in the precarious dawn, a homemade bicycle trailer and a bright yellow raincoat.

Josephine was on foot, the size of her territory limited by the two canvas bags she normally carried herself. From the age of ten on she never failed to get satisfaction by completing her route before school. On weekends carrying that feeling to Prince, the colt she had bought with the money earned. She describes Prince to Leo, uncharacteristically talkative when it comes to the fiercely loyal stallion she raised. And being a girl who knew the value of money, she got satisfaction watching his appraised value grow. Prince was going to put her through grad school.

Leo can barely keep up, shifting the heavy bag from shoulder to shoulder. The pressure of the strap penetrated his neck and spread numbness down his arm. A church standing at the crux of the figure eight she's created out of her paper route is where she leaves one bag, to be picked up on the way back.

They've just started and Leo is already tired. Handing papers to her apprentice, she points to the house, to put it in a box or push it through a slot. Even being slowed down by the need to instruct Leo on the finer points of delivery, she's still fast. Trying to pick up the pace, she leads him into apartment buildings with lobby mirrors where Leo is startled by how old he looks skulking along behind the weightless Josephine. They trudge down endless halls, drop papers at identical doors, take the elevator to the next floor. They hunt up suite numbers Josephine carries in her head.

In one building after another he notices the chemical smell, which the tenants are undoubtedly oblivious to. It could be insecticide or the decomposition of construction materials into mustard gas or the plastic plants putting out pheromones to attract the dust.

It's past seven when they finish and Josephine is apprehensive about Leo's ability to do the route himself. Stupefied, he watches the spilled paint sunrise, enhanced a thousandfold by bad work completed. He tells her not to worry. She has a new job at the university library, in the windowless sub-basement, which she can't afford to pass up.

Next morning his alarm clock starts chirping at four. He checks it against his watch. It can't be right, he just closed his eyes. Dropping back into the shallow grave of the sagging mattress, flirting with the ether of unreliability, he nearly falls back to sleep. But he's awake and disturbed at the notion of degradation being an arousal.

The memory of yesterday's sunrise motivates him to get on his feet and to put something in his stomach. Not wanting to disappoint Josephine gets him out the door. At first the brisk walk brings him up a notch but soon he's lost and he circles several blocks unnecessarily. By the time he locates the garage he's hopelessly last and fumbling helplessly to break apart the bundles, having forgotten the most important thing Josephine told him to remember, a knife. Lucky for Leo, the diffident supervisor keeps a box cutter in his car. Panic pushes its dull blade into his solar plexus and he sets off, carrying both bags as far as the church, then starting out, the sky already hinting at the kind of days it's going to be.

The streets all look the same and house numbers don't jibe. He puzzles over the map Josephine drew from memory last night. His progress is mostly sideways with mistakes doubtlessly occurring but with no time to fret. The faster he tries to go the more resistance he has to overcome and by seven he's only half done and already encountering the irate housecoats whose mornings he's ruined. Diligently slap-dash now, he tosses papers onto porches hoping good neighbours make good neighbours and he finally finishes long after the sun has risen. He goes home and utterly to bed, laying complete waste to the day.

Leo rolls over and looks at the clock. Someone's knocking. Quarter to midnight. Josephine's standing there in a ragged nightshirt.

There's a call for you, she says.

Christ.

Your friend, what's-her-name.

It's twelve-thirty when he walks out the door. Under the wet glare of lamplight he ploughs through the piles of fallen leaves. With all his experience and the specialized skills he's learned, it was still impossible for him to say no to a woman. His resolve was a fluid thing, and if he wasn't so lonely an hysterical phone call in the middle of the night might not seem so bitter.

June has been drinking, a lot. A cigarette dangles from one hand and she hands him a whisky with the other, then clears away some toys for him to sit down. He gets an empty feeling looking at his old space. He downs his drink and drops the glass on the rug. He puts an arm over her shoulder and pieces together the story of what happened, realizing maybe his arm there was inappropriate.

He takes a cigarette from her pack and lights up. He blows smoke rings.

Like riding a bike, he says. *Some things you never forget, eh?* He fills the air around her with milky circles, which she waves away.

I wish you wouldn't do that, she says.
Why?
It's irritating, and I don't have that many.
Sorry.

He puts it out and moves to the other end of the sofa.

I have to show you my poem, she says, dumping her purse out and sifting through the contents, her hair hanging over her face. He isn't sure if she's crying or just getting ready to pass out.

I know it's here, she rouses herself. *I wrote it at the bar. No one wanted to talk to me. I wrote it on something.*

Chequebooks, business cards, stock quotations, travel brochures. She examines it all with dramatic flair, as though her dignity was still salvageable. All he will ever be to a woman is an audience, a justification for another performance. She removes eyebrow pencils and lipgloss and combs and toys.

It's not here. Shit . . .

Leo watches her, wanting to bring her back, to make her present.

Sometimes I wish I was dead, he tells her, attempting to connect.

Do you? she asks.

Come here and cuddle. He pats the cushion and she obeys.

You're funny, he tells her, hoping to distract her, but she's too far gone.

Getting home he crawls into sleep, going unconscious almost immediately, simply forgetting to be awake. The sun slinks into his room around eight and he sits up. All over the city newspapers were dissected and coffee-ringed; but somewhere out there, Leo was almost certain, a man in a bathrobe was still waiting.

Leo stands in Josephine's door, watching her move the chapters of her thesis around on the unmade bed like a puzzle. In a book about time was chronology optional? She seems mature for her age, an old person in a new body. She was doing the paper route again and keeping the job at the library, but he's never seen her be goofy or outrageous on purpose.

Whatcha lookin' for? he asks.

It was here a minute ago, she muses.

What?

At first he found her strangeness unappealing but he's beginning to enjoy it. She forgets her wallet in stores, her textbooks on buses. She didn't rinse conditioner from her hair one morning and spent the whole day at school oblivious to it. She was missing a large section of her thesis when she got home one day and then a week later the missing piece appeared on the porch. The gods take pity on her.

You look like you need a beer, he says.

I can't.

What are you trying to do?

Make sense of it all.

Of black holes?

I could have been a vet.

Why didn't you?

They said I had potential to squander. I don't know
what that means.

Like I said. You look like you need a beer.

Oh . . .

Leo grabs his jacket and pats the pockets for his
wallet and keys. He wants to get high, hopefully
refresh his perspective on life. As they walk along he
senses her self-absorption, her unwillingness to let go
of her writing. He walks a little behind so he can
watch her profile. Framed by her big black hair, her
boyish face is interesting. Most women are afraid of
the hermaphrodite that lives under their make-up,
their dominant feature, for most of them, like nothing
from a magazine, galling and inescapable. He imagines
snuggling her and exploring her body, looking for the
hidden buds of eccentricity. Shifting his centre of gravity, he puts an arm over her shoulder. They walk along
dissimilar in rhythm and she shoulders him into a
hedge. He laughs and she reaches up to rub his neck.
Later in her bed he moves into her, with no smoke and
mirrors, no rituals of effort. There is a good chemistry
between them. He stops moving altogether, afraid of
spilling, perfectly balanced, like a cauldron tipped on

its edge. He whispers *don't move* and holds back the hair from her face. Her uniqueness mingles with his curiosity. Motion, stillness. Kicked by a gang of angels and left for dead. One cell at a time does Leo unwillingly come back to the land of the dead. He asks if she needs anything and she places his hand between her thighs. Sticky fruit, the frequency of bees, she gives in to the requirements of falling.

He lies beside her until his brain starts up with its inferior cast of characters. He stirs uneasily. He can't stay in her room. *I have to go*, he says.

'*Kay*, she mutters.

Clothes clutched to his body, the creaky stairs awaken underfoot. He lies on top of his covers, his body temperature dropping. At the bar she talked about black holes, event horizons and their geography. How time was spinning around a point in space, creating a situation where future and past could not exist. The orbit would eventually decay and be crushed down to a super-condensed time mass. She had only to think of a name for this material and her paper would be done. Leo became maudlin with too many beer, suggesting there was something like that in people's lives, a line they irretrievably crossed over. But Josephine just shrugged, unimpressed with his using her science as a metaphor.

Leo agrees to set the table for Lasha, though he's weary of being criticized for trivial things. He consults with her: Does she want the butter on a plate or in a dish? Should he use the long-stemmed glasses for water? She normally doesn't make a fuss on her night, but she's cooking something special, for him. He puts the napkins in rings and picks up a bouquet of carnations from the corner store, to counterbalance the criticism he's sure will come.

They habituate to their usual places at the table, Stephen just back from an excursion in the mountains sits beside Narayan; Daniel wearing billboard racing tights, and Josephine wearing a T-shirt inside out and backwards. Lasha brings in the large casserole and has Leo move the flowers to the sideboard so she can set it down. She removes the lid and releases a cloud of steam.

For Leo, she announces, *because he loves his mother.*

Leo remembers the kitchens of his childhood, recalls his mother's recipes, bragging how she could peel an apple in one long unbroken coil. He got poetic about Sunday roasts in the oven, the pressure cooker's counterbalance at full steam. He said he loved to sit beside the open window while she prepared an apple pie, the curtain fluttering a few inches from his face. There were chocolate chip crimes and mild scolding for the more serious transgression of climbing into her clothes hamper and hiding there to watch her undress. When the revelation of cellulite became his first disillusionment, he forgave her that and everything else, what all the women in his life had waited for in vain. Narayan unceremoniously starts the clockwise procession of food, beginning with the salad, passing it to Lasha.

Oh dear, she says, *never mind*.

Narayan passes the bread the wrong way and hands the steamed vegetables across the table to Daniel. He's too quick and too efficient and only causes chaos and confusion. Lasha tosses out the usual question: *What was everybody up to today?*

I was in the bush, Stephen says, looking around to see who cares. *Got some nice results.*

How is blowing something up art? Daniel asks.

How is it not art? Stephen retorts, not prepared to be challenged on such a basic level.

What's that supposed to mean?

What's it not supposed to mean?

Daniel shakes his head and eats.

I sold a box of books, Narayan says.

Do you keep explosives in the house? Daniel asks.

Stephen puts his fork down. This question has been asked before.

You need a blasting cap to set it off, he says. *I never have more than I'm going to use. That's how it is. Paperwork.*

Everyone is quiet for a few minutes, focussed on their hunger.

Why didn't the guy who invented the bomb get the

Nobel Prize in chemistry? Narayan asks Stephen, *When it was Nobel who invented high explosives.*

You don't see the grim reaper winning many Oscars, he answers.

Now there's a good actor, Josephine says, wanting a piece of their gibberish.

Better than Elvis? Narayan asks.

She is out of her depth.

Lasha says, *Leo set the table. Don't you think he did it beautifully?*

Hiroshima, would you call that art? Daniel persists, taking the conversation too personally.

I call a lot of things art.

That?

On TV, you know, Stephen struggles to be understood, *when they show the blast, and the shockwave is moving across the water towards the dummy ships, can you look away?*

I tried to set the table but who really knows how to set a table? Leo says.

The flowers were a nice touch, says Josephine.

After dinner, Daniel puts on his reflective gear and goes out for a ride. He won't be back for hours. In her leather jacket, her black curls brushed and big, Josephine heads out on a date, colour in her cheeks and a doubtful expression on her face. Narayan and Stephen head out somewhere, taking their endless debate for a walk. Leo is curious about their friendship. He hasn't had a male friend in years. Leo does the dishes and watches Lasha's hands fussing with the fringe on a new dress. He tosses the utensils into the drawer with a rhythmic clatter. As he dries the last of them, Lasha comes out of her room and her composure seems off-kilter, coy, which doesn't entirely suit her. A bottle of white wine appeared a few days ago which she now takes out of the fridge.

You're good with your hands, could you open this? She blanches at her awkwardness. He drives the coil into the cork while she takes two wine glasses down from the shelf.

You will join me?

He follows her to the dining room and watches her gather candles from around the room to the table where she can light them. She has a book of paper matches which bend and twist in her fingers. Leo has all but given up hope of her lighting one, but she manages, and coaxes a reluctant flame onto a wick and then it to the others.

I guess everyone's gone out, Leo says.

She finishes her wine and he pours her another.

You know . . . she begins, something on her mind.

What is it?

Her face is layered in transparencies: a suspicion, a question, misgivings, acceptance, resolve, kindness.

She says, *Salad bowls would have been nice.*

Oh?

You want to keep it away from the gravy, the salad.

He smiles. The tender hand of critique. He normally resents these pointless lessons in control, particularly after the fact, especially when he'd given her every opportunity to say something. Women have incredible memories when it comes to mistakes, but most men forget them as fast as they make them, because they don't automatically assume there is something inherently important at stake. And it's interesting to contemplate the world through the lens of oversight.

What are you thinking about? she asks.

I don't know much about you.

Is that important to you?

Only if you don't mind what I have to invent.

You almost sound angry at me.

He's jarred by the comment, confused, not wanting her to be right, not wanting her to see that part of him, unwilling to accept that there was anything to be angry about.

Have you ever been married? he asks, wanting to know at least that and thinking maybe there is a touch of frustration in his voice.

Men change their beliefs to suit the woman they're sleeping with, she says.

You saying they lie? Trying to sound more playful, more neutral. *Everybody lies*, he says.

It's not really lying then is it.

Narayan and Stephen return, bringing the smell of

outside in along with an aggressive contentment, flinging the door and shaking the house. Narayan comes through the dining room dangling a six-pack and goes to the sideboard for his favourite mug. Glancing doubtfully at the wine and the candles, he says, *Cheers*, smirking, and carries on into the kitchen where he opens two cans of beer and tosses the others in the fridge. On the other side of the kitchen he returns to the living room where Stephen is waiting to carry on with their conversation.

Baseball isn't intrinsically metaphysical any more than a chair is, Narayan is saying, in a carrying, badgering tone.

Or any less, Stephen replies.

But you can interpret anything in transcendental terms. If jump rope was their national sport there'd be books written about it too.

You're so full of shit. Stephen sounds drunk.

Come on, Lasha says to Leo, *let's go to my room.* He follows her with the wine and sits on her bed beside the dress she was working on. The geese get up out of their wicker bed on the floor and chatter mechanically for a few minutes.

Leo runs the back of his hand over the synthetic fabric of the dress, a lower temperature than his skin.

I paid two dollars for that one at the SPCA store.

Two dollars?

And it was on for half-price. Her hand lights on his shoulder as furtively as a butterfly.

She slides open her teak wardrobe and takes out a dress, holding it to herself as she stands between an oak-framed mirror beside the wardrobe and another on the bedroom door.

She takes another one down and throws the first one on the bed.

I like that one, he says, uncertain of the rules or even of the game.

What about this? she says, holding another one to herself.

Yah, definitely.

She stands between the mirrors, swishing and crimping, with hands that show her age. Through the multiplied reflections she is watching him.

Would you like to try one on? she says, continuing to study her reflections, now with another dress, watching Leo's reactions. He goes numb, always the obedient audience, nodding to her commentary about colours while his head buzzes with confusion over her question. Or did he not hear her right? He hears things that aren't there sometimes, or through a filter of paranoia that turns everything backwards. He discovers his hand in the bodice of one of the dresses beside him and the head of a goose hovers like a bee over a flower.

Lasha is suddenly tired and Leo moves so she can lie down.

Are you okay?

Sometimes I think I could sleep all the time.

Should I go?

Would you mind terribly?

You're worn out.

I just need to lie down for a while. She cups his cheek with a fragrant hand.

Narayan is standing beside the fridge scrutinizing Leo as he comes out of Lasha's room. Pulling the door until it latches, Leo catches the beer Narayan tosses to him. He wants to be alone but Narayan corrals him into the other room where he sits on the sofa and watches Narayan and Stephen talk back and forth while his thoughts wander back to Lasha's bed. She is a woman with much to be mined. The age difference alone elevates her to the realm of forbidden fruit, rife with the unknown, tastes to be acquired. In her apparent inexperience he imagines great depths of surprise. But therein lies the trap, the sticky petals that close on you. She would want a great romance, believing such a thing was possible, and would end up disappointed and hating him. She would flower into a schoolgirl, then whither at his first betrayal, her injured pride becoming a sarcophagus for his memory, sealing them in together for a thousand years.

When Josephine returns she seems relieved to be

out of the clutches of her juvenile friends. She plunks herself down next to Leo and nudges him playfully, her knee against his.

Just pure energy, Stephen is saying.

Yah, but what kind? Narayan asks.

All kinds, kinetic, chemical . . .

But that makes him no better than our slave.

So?

Narayan shakes his head bitterly. *I have read every scripture, new age or self-help, Hindu, Buddhist, The Bible. I have searched satsang, church, synagogue, the house of God, the whorehouse, the outhouse, the movie house. I have been to the mountain. So you can believe me when I tell you that I am sincere when I say there is no God.* Turning to Josephine, he adds: *Unless you call randomness a kind of default God, a kind of ideal monster, something to dress up with our moods.*

Why do you want to be God so bad if you claim he doesn't exist? asks Stephen.

You're drunk.

Josephine winks at Leo, *They're still at it, eh?*

Still going strong. I'm going to bed.

On his way through the kitchen Leo notices that Lasha's door is open a few inches. He could put his head in and see how she is, take it from there. But he's used up his daily quotient of self-confidence and instead goes up to bed. He reads for a while, rubbing his eyes against the words, distracted by his vague worries.

He turns the light out so he can fantasize about Lasha, about kissing her breathtakingly clean tongue, and putting on one of her dresses.

A little later his door opens and Josephine slips into his bed, dropping her nightshirt on the way. He is surprised and uncomfortable about it at first, but she wiggles herself into his arms and pooh-poohs his excuses. Like water merging with water they meld and pass through one another until they're lying back to back.

Into his awareness comes the sounds of tree frogs and crickets, and the Morse code of curious birds, the distinct squeak of the top step, and someone standing outside his door. A gentle knock, *Leo?* The door swings open and Little One comes through followed by Ophelia. They proceed to explore under the bed and Josephine lifts herself on an elbow to see what's going on. Leo closes his eyes. *The girls just wanted to say goodnight, Leo? Are you awake?* A sudden intake of breath. *Oh, I'm sorry,* in a whisper. The birds continue their explorations of Leo's room while Lasha calls them from the bottom of the stairs.

In the morning Leo goes to social services. He grabs up a magazine as he drops into a chair. Flipping pages so well thumbed they have the feel of old dollar bills. People in bad coats occupy the chairs around him. They probably know more than Leo does about how the system works, the right buttons to push. An anorexic woman appears with his folder under her arm. Down the hall in front of him goes her skinny ass and if there's one button he understands it's the one she swivels on. Her office is a plain affair with room enough for her desk and two chairs. She'll be a hard one to crack, he can tell, as she crosses her legs.

What can I do for you . . . Mister? she scans his file.

Leo, call me Leo.

Leo. No smile, tight as a clam shell.

Outside the window a bird is trying to crack something open by dropping it from high above onto the pavement.

When's the last time you were in Hawaii? he asks.

Excuse me?

Hawaii, he goes on. *Judging by your tan I'll bed you just got back, not, what, two months ago?* He smiles.

I've never been. She's not interested in being friendly, though his subliminal substitution of *bed* has left her a little dazed.

I don't believe that for a minute.

It's a nice place, I hear, she says, relaxing a notch up to neutral.

For a woman like you it's paradise. He takes her in his talons and carries her up. *You'd never want to leave. It would be just you, and . . . And? What do you like to do? Read, play Boggle?*

Sounds nice, she warms up to the image.

And what have we got to look forward to here?
I don't know.
Cold hard pavement.
Ouch.

Four hundred and ten dollars is not enough, he says, squirming in his chair, pulling out the stops. His adolescent routine always works on tight-assed women. He rakes his hair and slumps a little further into the chair. She gives up a faint smile.

My rent is almost three hundred, he says, *and then there's my hydro, my phone, and then what do I eat, or how do I pay for my bus pass, or take a pretty woman to the movies?*

Have you thought about getting a cheaper place to live?
What's cheaper than $275?
I don't know.
You tell me where and I'll run right over.
I wouldn't know.
Who would?
Is there anything else I can do for you?
Anything else? You haven't done anything yet.
What do you want me to do?
I need more money.
There's nothing I can do about that.
What do you do around here then?
You're a single, employable male, she says, referring to her book.

But I can't live on that.

If there's nothing else?

Damn it! he says, his composure snarled up. His body language expressing something that pushes her back into her chair.

Walking home he feels sick and empty. He doesn't know if he needs to eat something or to vomit. He needs to sit in his room and shut the door and not come out for a day or two. But when he gets there he can't do that, because his clothes and his books and all his stuff is out on the sidewalk, haphazardly thrown down, as shocking as a corpse. He has to look away, feeling insulted. He thinks he should react, in case someone is watching, throw a fit or start shouting, but neither of those seem to match the situation. What does? He looks around the neighbourhood at the comatose houses, where no one is watching, where no one is ever watching. His scaffolding pride crumples around his feet and he just stands there waiting for the first breeze to knock him over. He wants to congratulate himself. It confirms what he's always known. It rings true.

From one of the boxes he lifts out his tool belt, limp as a dead dog. The house stares blankly like an animal. Where no curtains move, another queasy ending. He studies the grey sky. He could take his room back, occupy it by force, demand his rights under the law, but for some reason this was easier, to just walk away. Picking up the boxes in his arms and dragging the green bags behind him he goes down the alley, calculating the dreadful relative value of things, tossing items into cans, the least important first, as though these distinctions existed anymore.

For years he studiously kept it simple, whittling away at what accumulated. His marriage was a magnet for junk and their garage was to the rafters with dollar store accessories and defective Christmas trees. His shaving kit, his books, his alarm clock, into a dumpster with his runners and his brogues. He shucks hurry from off his shoulders. His brooding destination seems to be the bridge. In his newly ethereal existence it seemed the steadiest thing around.

Into a parks board trash can go his birth certificate, driver's license, library card, his ten-year AA chip— dog tags from all manner of armies of the mundane. The picture of his son he feeds the worms in a flowerbed. All that remained was his tool belt, and the few items he stuck in the pockets: reading glasses, a comb, a pen.

When he gets to the bridge he finds art students filming something. Two young men with pig shaves and goatees are directing a female who is falling out of her hooker's dress and sitting awkwardly to one side while they shoot some object they've deemed more worthy: the Matryoushka doll. Sitting down nearby Leo closes his eyes. He's disappointed the doll turned out to be only a prop. Was this Stephen's afterlife in art, where everything is turned into a movie backdrop, even Vancouver's turbid winter?

His narratives are snarled, the voices in his head are pure gibberish. To calm himself he thinks about sex with the young actress, but he can't lock onto an image, can find no memories of touch. He doesn't remember drifting off but he is suddenly chilled and the students have vanished. A trench coat is going down the trail, navy pantyhose semaphore, a woman pretty by lipstick. She clutches a disposable lighter and a brown nine-by-eleven. Leo had an impressive well-paid wife who could walk faster than any man he knew. She'd burst about the house on her short legs, doing more in an hour than Leo normally did in a week.

Distractedly yanking weeds out of the dirt he finds cigarette remains and tosses them away, but there are so many, filters the colour of gravel. Decades of men have been throwing stones at bottles down here, men waiting for their number to come up, men leaning against the wall smoking. You saw them in holocaust films, the last currency of the damned.

Fifteen dollars and change is all he's got left for food, and all he can think about is having a cigarette.

Masts of sailboats slip over the lawn. From somewhere the sound of an electric sander. The West End rises like a cemetery on the north shore of False Creek. People don't understand themselves anymore;

they can't read their own messages, their alignments to stars and clockwork superstitions just make them vulnerable. The day moves oddly, each moment is distinct, but the spaces between them vary in length. One minute can't end soon enough, then *wham*, two hours have passed.

He walks as far as MacDonald and back via the alleys. Behind the thrift store he finds a blanket. Back at the bridge he huddles next to a support column. By moonlight he studies his hands. The skin so porous, so dubious. Scar tissue seems like different skin, smoother, more articulate. He's thankful for the blanket. It consolidates his worries into one easy payment of getting through the night.

Five

JUNE THOUGHT LAWYERS were supposed to have glass offices with brass lettering. This one has cracked plaster walls and waiting room chairs scrounged from the dump. An elegant Asian woman stands before her, smiling, hand outstretched.

Call me Enny, she says.

June shakes her hand, but doesn't smile, can't smile with the broken tooth that makes her look like some kind of washout. Once in the woman's office, June immediately starts in on her story. She needs to make somebody understand. Enny listens, her face calm and serious, while June gets more and more flustered, her story coming out all wrong, details getting mixed up, contradictions staring back from every conclusion.

I think you've been poorly treated by everyone concerned, says Enny.

Do you think so?

I do.

Thank god somebody understands.

Exactly when did you assault the social worker?

I didn't assault her, really. I pushed her, hard. I wanted to kill her.

This was after they took your son?

Yes.

Social workers are supposed to be prepared to deal with angry people. Enny's voice is slow and musical. *They can't really expect anything else, can they, taking a child away from its mother?*

So why am I being charged?

Maybe she's been attacked once too often, and decided to take it out on you. I'd say that's pretty likely. She doesn't like you, personally, that's clear. Is she seriously injured? I doubt it, though according to their lawyer she's in a neck brace.

What's going to happen to me?

Unknown.

Will I go to jail?

Not if there is a god in heaven.

Do you go to church?

It would help our cause if you considered a rehabilitation program.

I don't think that's a good idea.

Why?

I don't know.

I don't see that we've got much choice.

A nurse, a pharmacist, three housewives, a doctor, a truck driver, losers and liars. Bleary-eyed and unsettling, human fragility's cringing rank and file. They introduce themselves around the circle, say a little about how they got into whatever drug of choice they were hooked on. When it comes June's turn to show-and-tell her defects and defeats she protects the truth. This is not a safe place for it, though she knows it's supposed to be. Outrageously, she tells them she was brought down by sobriety, not substance abuse, that drugs helped her focus and made her a rich woman.

The program leaders glance at one another. Margaret, a would-be striking redhead—if not for an off-putting lack of humour—and Mike, a lugubrious former charmer, all but vanquished behind a transluscent grin. It's clear they have read her file. She's screwed already.

After the first-day orientation, mornings begin with a group meditation at eight sharp. Margaret leads them through a field of cows beside a babbling brook: fluffy clouds drift in the sky, a breeze, birds. June feels frustrated and watches the others follow the visualization, their eyes clamped, brows knit, except for one woman who is grinning back at June. A young woman in the way June is youngish; pretty, in the way June is okay pretty. She can't remember her name. Jean? On the third day June makes sure to sit beside her.

Next morning June excludes herself from Margaret's meditation and hangs around the outer office thumbing through brochures and staring at herself in an unflattering mirror, horrified by the woman staring back at her. She lost a tooth on one of her last binges and it makes her look worse than she could have ever imagined.

Mike is afraid of Margaret and he watches her for his cues to do his bit, which includes a session in front of a video camera. He cuts two participants at a time from the group and takes them to the other end of the room. He puts June in front of the camera and Jean in the chair opposite.

The point, he tells them, *is for you to see your own body language. To see what other people see, the kinds of messages you convey nonverbally. This is part of the "learning to communicate effectively" portion of the program.* He puts the last bit in quotes to prove he's really one of them and ineptly fumbles with the controls on the camera. June finds him repulsive, men should be good at these things.

Once rolling and satisfied the tripod isn't going to fall over, he asks June pre-scripted questions, stupid ones to start, like the names of family members, then onto harder ones, like her opinion on the question of world hunger. When she gives a standard answer to the impossible question he challenges her for not doing something about it. She gets flustered and defensive and forgets about the camera. She makes up excuses and contradicts herself and gets quite uncomfortable. Then Mike leans closer to her and asks how it feels when men tell her how beautiful she is. She feels hit on and answers with an angry stillness. Men are such flies.

Mike rewinds the tape and they watch it. June is appalled by how ill at ease she looks, like she's got bugs crawling all over her.

Why do I have to look at this? I hate myself.

He assures her that it's common for people to react negatively when they see themselves as others do for the first time.

Oh, that makes me feel a lot better.

When the tape gets to his last question, or was it a flirtation, June looks angry but calm as well, and sharp, like she's ready to unhinge her jaw and swallow him whole. He smiles like she's supposed to think he did it on purpose.

She works hard at staying positive about the program, getting up in the morning with a sense of purpose and coming home in the afternoon with something accomplished. She's dealing more effectively with normal daily irritations and the bigger picture seems less tragic. However, the last few months are still a blur. She doesn't remember much after they gave sole custody to Rick, just the coke and the money down the drain, the hangovers. One night she woke up in someone's garden all scratched and torn. Another time she found herself in Port Coquitlam on a bus with some jerk who seemed to think they were friends.

June takes a day off the program to get her tooth fixed. She picks a dentist from the Yellow Pages because her own guy was a family friend and a gossip. The assistant pushes a floor pedal, rising and unbending June from sitting to supine, then adjusts the light out of her eyes. It's not true what they say about the eyes being windows to the soul. With the hieroglyphics of muscle and bone hidden behind a surgical mask, they're just marbles, cat's eyes. A smiling tooth and a talking toothbrush stare down at her from the ceiling. She reads and rereads the captions, trying to occupy her mind, as the hawk-eyed old dentist builds a dam in her mouth. Then he constructs a new tooth with an acrylic paste the assistant mixes, which he packs onto the prepared stump, working to stay a step ahead of the hardening. He scrapes and shapes and fires up a drill with a planet-sized bit. He works a strip of abrasive between the reborn tooth and its survivor, yanking June's head back and forth. Time crawls over broken glass. Desperation beats like a trapped bird on a window. Suddenly it's over and the assistant kicks the floor pedal. A drill in the next cubicle shrieks, and June is sent dizzy into the street.

Margaret comes up with an exercise she calls "positive reckoning." For it she places a chair at the centre of the circle and asks for a volunteer. A housewife who recently confessed to being a hooker puts up her hand, eager for more of the truth. But her face nearly drops off when Margaret lobs the first question at her to show the others how it works.

Do you think it was good that your parents found out you were a hooker the way they did?

The poor woman is stunned.

Why did you abandon your children? one of the men asks.

The questions bounce off their targets, but not without doing their damage. Even such gems as: *What's the matter with you, anyway?* are acceptable to Margaret.

June has stayed quiet throughout the game. When it's her turn to take the hot seat she crosses her arms and refuses.

Please, June, Mike pleads, to keep the peace, knowing Margaret and June have bad chemistry between them.

June pities the man, his passionate belief in harmony, the way he pulls his punches, the way he defers to women and despises men. He wants to get somewhere and keeps moving straight for it, but there's a closed window in front of him, and he keeps bumping his head. He appeals to her, believing there's a connection between them. His dreary flirtation has bought him a piece of her and she doesn't know why that has to be so. She stands up slowly and wearily sits where they all want her to sit.

The questions start out simple.

What are you afraid of? somebody asks.

None of your business, June replies.

Come on, tell us what you're afraid of, somebody insists.

June has to compose herself, then says, *Same as you, I guess. Everything.*

When did you give up on life?

This was Margaret's question, and it digs like an elbow.

I didn't give up.

Sure you did. You said screw it, screw them all.

I'm not going to sit here and listen to this.

Are you going to give up again?

That's what you want, June says, accusing Margaret, trying to draw her out so she can shoot her down, to confirm what she already knows, what they all know, that June's a piece of crap, that she'll take any excuse to hurt herself.

Of course that's not true, Margaret says.

I knew this was a bad idea, June says, looking for Jean but coming back to Margaret and seeing something she most definitely did not want to see, kindness.

This is shit, June proclaims, snatching her coat off the chair and storming out. She flings the door closed behind her, expecting it to shake the walls, but a cushion of air turns the gesture back, lodging it in her neck.

Later she calls Gunther to say goodnight. He is full of the things he did that day, and he makes June feel better. They talk for half an hour before he goes to bed. His dad takes the phone and wants to chat for a while, just like they were old friends, as if he wasn't the biggest prick of them all. And so she chats, because she has to, because the situation gives her no choice; she knows it and he knows it.

She goes into the kitchen to see who's knocking on the door.

You should have seen the look on her face, Jean squeals as she comes in, taking a swing around the apartment, checking out the bedroom, glancing at the shelves.

She turned red like she was going to faint, or cry, and was gone for the rest of the day. Wanna drink?

You're kidding?

I stopped on my way over. I thought you might be needing something.

You're amazing.

June puts out glasses and Jean pours out equal shots of vodka.

You got a spoon I can use?

What for?

Jean lays a small, ziplock bag of white powder and a syringe on the table.

I hope you don't mind, but I have to. You probably hate me.

I don't hate you.

She turns the powder into liquid and draws it into the chamber of the syringe. Holding it up to the light she taps it with a fingernail. So calm, these moments before a fix.

Want some?

I couldn't.

But you want to.

I want a lot of things I can't have.

Like?

June doesn't answer.

Jean injects herself. It looks so simple.

Jean reads June's thoughts, says *If you don't want it, you don't want it.*

I've never injected anything before, and I don't want to start.

Believe me, I know where you're coming from.

The syringe lays on the table and June lights a cigarette.

What do you say? Jean is no longer willing to play the patience game. *I know you want to. There's no point in denying it.*

I don't deny it.

It won't kill you.

Show me how.

The sexiness of the idea, the expanding inside, just from the promise. But the needle lies and that feeling of being bad turns into lethargy and is definitely not worth it. She's crossed into new territory and doesn't recognize the landmarks, the blue cherry on her arm, the junky in her kitchen. Aware of her awesome lack of self-knowledge, June settles into a grim calm. The absence of references becomes the first reference.

Leo scratches his beard and looks out at the morning. It taunts him with impossible challenges and trivial glories. It's not raining yet at least. He wraps his blankets in plastic and stows them in a crevice with his tool belt. There's been more rain than usual. Or has there? Living outside you notice every fluctuation, every drop of temperature, every pungent steam release from Molsons, every poisonous discharge from the body shops nearby. The kind of day it is doesn't matter though because it's laundry day, the best day of the week.

The windows of the laundromat are dirty on the outside and on the inside they have a layer of film. The wall around the pay phone is scaly with business cards and ads for lost animals. A pair of pants, a shirt, and two pairs of socks hardly constitutes a load, but it's worth it. Just knowing he has something clean to put on can get him through the most degrading days. The machine obeys instantly when he plugs it with two hard-earned quarters. Obedient old technology. He adds soap to the rising water and breathes the comforting steam.

He'd like to sit in one of the plastic chairs and splurge with a machined coffee, forget his life for one slice of time. But he has to keep moving, for the privacy of movement, for the aluminum cans and plastic bottles. He is placated by the heat of work and stops to investigate a broken figurine in the dirt and a teaspoon run over by a thousand station wagons. Later the dumpster divers will come to life and in twenty-minute intervals will cover the same territory, lifting the heavy lids with a cursory glance in and letting them crash closed with all the finesse of a car accident. Leo has improved on their system. He wears gloves and latches the dumpster open, tearing into bags and shifting the top layer around. Considerate of people living nearby, he sets the heavy lids down gently. Back at the laundromat he transfers his things to the dryer. Again he's tempted to sit down. A *People* magazine beckons.

He treks residential alleys, searches the long grass between garages, finds a dozen beer cans in the stairwell of a school, then circles back to pick up his clothes. He takes them back to the bridge and eats an orange that had fallen to the sidewalk outside a produce store. Then he sets out in earnest. Alleys run east and west making travel south impractical, which is why he seems to have Kerrisdale to himself.

In a blue box he finds a recycling schedule that contains useful information about holidays and long weekends. The tricky part is knowing which end to start at to beat the ferocious chiming of boxes being emptied into the truck. The pristine alleys are deserted and tall fences blot out the embassies of debt. He can go hours without encountering a soul. It's like the end was nearer than anybody expected and nobody thought to mention it to him.

Concealing his day's work behind a hedge, he goes into a coffee shop, taking one of the sagging bench seats in the booth beside a large fish tank. Odd clumsy species drift in the algae light. He's got a lot of walking to do yet. The depot is at Ontario and Seventh, north-east, a few more miles at least. He has a coffee and a refill and then gets moving.

He sorts the plastic from the aluminum and the cashier takes his word for it and pays him in cold cash. A good end to a decent day, for a few dollars.

Going into a fast-food place, he orders fries and a hamburger. With some satisfaction in the hard seat under him, he sets himself in front of an abandoned newspaper. He eats slowly and stares out the window at the ant farm of humanity. Isn't something supposed to happen? Armageddon? The personal ads all sound the same: likes to read and go for long walks. But Leo wonders if two loners together make a couple. In the Living section he reads that science is about to double the human life span.

As long as I don't start talking to myself.

In a bus shelter he finds a valid transfer and rides to

the end of the line and back, slumped on the jiggling seat, revelling in the fabricated smell of dryness.

Back at the bridge it's dark and dank. He drags a ladder out of concealment and climbs onto his ledge, pulling it up behind him. He has four blankets, two for underneath and two for over. For his head, a small cushion that smells. Tomorrow he'll wear clean clothes, maybe blow some money on a pair of earplugs, the kind you squeeze, that expand in your ears. Why don't bridges sleep?

Was it an accident, a run at his limitations, to be made an example of by the fates? He didn't abuse his luck or cut it with risk or do serious drugs. He had too many ways of looking at things. What did Benny mean by killing himself?

He drifts off until something scraping about beneath him brings him around. A rat chewing into somebody's dream? He hears voices, a dim fluttering. Maybe a hooker working or somebody looking for him, for Leo. But that's ridiculous. Listen to the rubber rain, stare at the photonegative night. The voices stay in their orbit. He relaxes a little, thinks about his son. What could have been strong enough to hold him? Then the concussion of a gunshot echoes under the bridge, from pillar to pillar, a tearing sound. It voids the moment, starts everything over with a drumming heart.

As morning seeps in under the bridge, the sky turning from licorice grey to ash, Leo lowers the ladder. Damp cold intensifies the pungency of the blackberry bushes. Long grasses bend under the weight of dew. At five in the morning traffic overhead is steady. He paces to get warm and keeps an eye on the trails for the criss-cross of pedestrians, which will be his cue.

The gunshot from last night still echoes. It was a gunshot. It could have been nothing else. There were voices in and around it and lesser sounds indistinguishable from the crackling and popping of his nerves. Then he sees it, a body. Fully awake now, he kneels, thinking it is a woman, his heart squeezing into his throat. But it's a man with a silk shirt and five-hundred-dollar shoes. The face is a snapshot, an anxious portrait of devotion to one holding the camera. His shoes are scuffed and the ground is scraped, like he tried to get up and walk home. He would have understood his body then, and the white light. He would have laid aside with dwindling regret the butterflies on his shirt. Leo touches the skin of the mask with the backs of his fingers, gone out, not translucent.

The bullet entered through the left ear and didn't exit. The sandy soil has drained the blood away with barely a trace. In the dead man's wallet he finds three twenty-dollar bills. What does it mean to rob a corpse? Surely etiquette has something to say about such transgressions. They are a different species, their words leave us cold, their money feels fake.

Leo collects his stuff from the ledge. The police will swarm. They'll go over the area with their dogs and cameras and scratch their shaved chins. A jogger coming down the trail has stopped and is reaching for something in her back pocket. Leo makes for the stairs and on the bridge he looks up towards the backdrop of downtown towers where the cars gnash and grind. He decides against it, instead chancing across six lanes of rush hour traffic, waking up a few hundred drivers. On the other side of the bridge he slips down the east abutment and is back where he started.

From the window of her new office June can see the glass towers of Howe Street, if she twists just so and stands on her toes. May is her new partner, a woman she's known from when she first got into the industry, though it wasn't until they met at an AA meeting that they became friends. It seemed natural when May and June talked about starting their own company, working for themselves, and they came up with the name, Spring Promotions. They rent the office by the month and share a large table for a desk. June bought some frameless prints for the walls and May brought a large dusty rhododendron from home. As well as Trend

Recreational Developments, which June brought into the partnership, they promote El Niño Silver and Bullwest Minerals, with new clients on the way. Their investor base is small but dedicated, true believers.

It's a lot of work keeping a twelve-cent stock at fifteen. It's all news releases and bullshit. When her eyes glaze over with fatigue, June stares at the deranged telephone pole in the lane outside their second-floor window, all awry like a burst fishing reel, but with an underlying order she can't put her finger on. Travelling squirrels pause in front of the jumble, before heading off towards the park or west to god knows where.

George Kaslikoff, the owner of Trend, who goes even further back with June, is thinking of buying property on Lost Lake, an old homestead with fishing lodge potential. He has the deal spread all over their desk.

What you're looking at, ladies, is a treasure map. And right there, he says, pointing to a spreadsheet, *is the X that marks the spot. Look at that number, and this one.*

Interesting, says May, looking at his fingers, the cluster of diamonds on his pinkie.

And look at this prospectus.

Whoa!

Are there any fish in the lake? June asks.

You've hit the nail on the head, Lover.

Don't call me that.

How quick can you two pack?

Excuse us?

How does three days in the sunny Okanagan sound?

It's winter.

And don't bring too much stuff, my car hasn't got much of a trunk.

You bought the Porsche? May asks.

What do you need us for? June wants to know.

Kaslikoff gives her a withering look. *Do you know what the secret of success is?* he asks.

Fishing?

Listening, he says, watching her face as she comprehends his meaning.

She says, *What makes you think I know anything about fishing?*

He shakes his head in a familiar, irritating way, *How long have we known each other?*

When June was a girl her father, Jerry, took her fishing. From Spanish Banks they'd plane out over English Bay, past the rusting freighters and racing bathtubs, to the south end of Bowen Island or the mouth of the Capilano River, where he'd cut the Merc and let them drift, while he showed her what to do. He'd start the trolling engine and their drifting would become focussed drifting. He taught her to listen to the out-running line, to feel it flutter in her hand, to know where she was. He showed her how to watch for weather, said the ocean only respected those with the guts to steer into the storm, away from illusions of safety. But he was killed on the highway, running head-on into another pickup towing a boat. He was always saying things like that.

In the afternoon of the next day Kaslikoff pulls up at June's place with May already in the car. He honks and June comes out with an overnight bag, which he tosses in the trunk beside May's suitcase and his huge sports tote. She shakes her head and climbs in beside May and groans, realizing they have to share a seat.

Spitting gravel, they turn onto Twelfth Avenue and head for the freeway. The wind whips their hair into their eyes as they pull their jackets tight.

That's the last time I spend eighty bucks on my hair, May says.

What's the use of having a convertible if you don't convert?

Put the top up for fuck sake, George, June says.

He slows down, congesting the cars behind as he pulls over. He walks around the Boxster trying to attach the roof and, getting frustrated with a clasp, he begins to sulk.

Men should not be allowed to own status automobiles, June remarks. *They are more vain than women.*

They have a good laugh and Kaslikoff grins back at them like a fool. June gets out to help.

On the freeway, touchy brake lights stretch for miles. This surging and suddenness goes on for hours before traffic thins out past Mission. By dusk Kaslikoff is drawn and tired-looking and June is desperate to pee.

They pull off at a rest area and get out of the car to stretch. The cement floor of the unheated building amplifies the scraping of sand under June's shoes, and it galls her to put her bare ass on the cold seat. She pushes the flusher with her foot.

Kaslikoff produces a bag of powder from under the driver's seat.

I didn't know you were bringing that shit, June says.

Hey, relax. He rolls a ten-dollar bill into a tube.

I'm not sure it's sanitary to put money in your nose, says May.

Who's first?

Kaslikoff has renewed energy for driving and the day closes down until nothing exists out the beams of their headlamps. June rolls the window down for the clean air and watches the vague shapes of her thoughts rush past. They pull off on a lookout above Okanagan Lake and look at Kelowna sparkling like a forest fire on the other side. Driving into town they find an unpromising-looking bar and go in search of something to eat. Kaslikoff steers them to a vacant table and scrounges some chairs that men in black T-shirts are using as footstools.

A woman with a tray comes over.

What can I get you folks?

Menus?

And three draught.

And a ginger ale, June says.

May whispers, *This is a horrible place.*

It's a classic, says Kaslikoff.

I don't want to stay, says June.

The beers are coming.

Fuck the beers.

It's rustic. You get a feel for small towns.

This isn't a small town.

It used to be.

June says, *Give me the keys. I'll wait in the car.*

Come on, what are you afraid of?

She holds out her hand and Kaslikoff relents.

If the car's not there when you come out . . . June is too angry. She strides out of the place, with May close on her heels.

She starts the car and lets May in the other side.

That man is such a fucking jerk, June cries.

Kaslikoff raps on the window, *Let me in.*

When they turn off the highway, Kaslikoff slows down to locate a new rattle from inside the car, putting his hands on knobs and panels, nearly driving off the road reaching under the dash to check the fuse box lid. When they find the store with the gas pump he was watching for, he starts looking for other signs indistinctly remembered: a fork in the road, a turn to the left. He counts driveways and mailboxes, letting the car drift to a stop as he considers a particularly dark lane. Branches claw miserably at the sides of the car as Kaslikoff pulls down a long neglected driveway.

Pulling up to a large log house, he turns the lights off, kills the engine, and rolls the windows down to sit in the stillness. In the darkness somewhere nearby Lost Lake is breathing and a gust of wind rattles a loose gate, reminding June of something, transporting her to the small hospital in the Fraser Valley where the ambulance had taken Jerry after his accident. She and her mother had spent the night beside him, listening to him die, noting every unconscious click and gasp. It was a nightmare within a nightmare and when he finally stopped breathing neither of them registered it for a while, the silence being too precious to interrupt with mourning.

Kaslikoff and May find their way to the back door and try to determine in the dark which is the right key. June stretches and walks around to the side of the house and looks at the luminous Milky Way, amazed by how much it resembles a city in the air. A little farther on, the reflecting lake, visible through the trees, outlines the dark shape of a boathouse.

She goes back around and finds Kaslikoff and May inside the house, groping around for a light switch.

If we're going to spend the night in the dark I need another line, May declares, apparently hooked already.

Fuck, Kaslikoff says.

What's the matter?

*I flicked the wrong switch. I think I just shut down
the generator.*

What generator?

The one that keeps the dam closed.

What dam?

Shit. Do you feel that?

Feel what?

The vibration.

What is it?

*Millions of gallons of water. The house is right in its
path.*

Okay, asshole.

June cries out, *Shit! What was that?*

May finds the right switch and the lights come up.
Hanging around them from hooks on the walls and
from racks on the ceiling glitter the makings of a well-
equipped kitchen.

I cut myself on something, June tells them.

Where's the bathroom? May wonders.

One down here and another upstairs.

Are there any bandages?

There's a bottle of scotch in my bag.

May locates the scotch and holds it up to the light
of the porch to reassure herself that it's full.

In the main room are pictures from the '40s. You
can't tell much about the former owners: if he hit her,
or they drank. Intelligent and in love is how they

look, but ghosts don't photograph. Kaslikoff leans on the mantel beside a stuffed owl and tells what he knows, that they passed away within weeks of each other. The walls are full of useful and useless things from other places and other times, stuff that should have been thrown out ages ago, a piece of lava rock, an artillery shell casing, a leg-hold trap, a picture of Churchill. When there's no room left for anybody else's curses, what then?

June makes up a bed in one of the rooms and stares at herself in the window wondering what happened. She used to have optimism and good skin. Nothing ever seems to pan out. Friends and money come and go and before you know it there's some cartoon character who stole your wallet standing in your place. She lies down and imagines the pressure of someone else on the bed. Didn't she believe it when Jerry told her he could get out of any predicament the weather could throw at him, because of his knack for untangling problems, returning with solutions.

She takes her make-up into the bathroom where the light is better and fixes herself up, although her mood spoils the effect. She pulls the skin around her eyes, wondering if a face-lift would change anything.

Kaslikoff and May are having a drink when June comes down.

I didn't know you could cook, meaning either of them.

There are literally hundreds of cans in the cellar, Kaslikoff says, manic from the cocaine. *You have to come down and have a look, it's so survivalist. But have a drink first. You're far too grumpy to appreciate it.*

I'm not grumpy, June says.

Do you see any social workers here? he says.

Where'd they keep the fishing rods?

They eat in silence and Kaslikoff finishes first. Leaning on the back legs of his chair, he watches the women through glazed eyes.

Why do women eat so slow?

Because they aren't pigs?

They're pigs in other ways, he says.

June and May look at each other.

What are we going to do tonight? he asks.

Got to be a deck of cards around here somewhere.

June clears the dishes and when May leaves the room to see what she can find, Kaslikoff traps June against the sink.

What are you doing?

Imagine finding you here, with me.

Imagine that. She escapes and cleans the table.

What's the problem?

There's no problem, it's just that I'm not interested.

He smiles in a way she finds irritating, the way he gloats about everything. The fact that he's making millions, mostly in gold stocks, just makes him that much uglier.

May returns from the big room with a Monopoly game and sets it up on the kitchen table. Kaslikoff wins the toss and goes first, moving his token to VER-MONT AVENUE.

I'll buy that, he says.

That piece of crap? says May.

This is a game, he says. *Try to remember that.*

Everything's a game, says June, *and nothing's a game.*

Ooh, the philosopher.

June gets the ELECTRIC COMPANY while May picks up CONNECTICUT AVENUE.

Kaslikoff brings out more drugs.

While you're up, he says to May, *fix a round of scotches?*

I'm not up.

My mistake.

May sighs and gets up for glasses.

What I wouldn't give for a cigarette, June says.

Go get some. Take my car. We passed that store, remember?

You'd let me drive your car?

I'd let you drive it, you know that.

Never mind, I don't need one that bad.

Take a ride on the Reading Railroad, Kaslikoff says.

I wanted the railroads, May moans.

They pause to do more cocaine, a line each for the women and two for Kaslikoff.

Okay, where were we? You guys ready for fishing tomorrow? Pay Luxury Tax. Fuck! Go ahead June, your turn. Doc Sprattly's my favourite fly. Favourite lure is the Deadly Dick. That really is one, you know. I didn't just make that up.

June lands on BOARDWALK.

Fuck! I wanted Boardwalk, he yells.

And then May acquires PARK PLACE.

Ever play strip Monopoly?

Two hundred please, for passing GO, June says to May.

Me, too, two hundred please.

For what?

I don't think I collected last time.

Sure you did?

I don't think I did.

You did. I'm positive.

I don't remember collecting it.

Trust me.

Trust a banker?

Gimme your keys, says June. *Don't play while I'm gone.*

She puts the key in the ignition and organizes her limbs around the controls. The illusion of competence is important. Driving along the lake for a mile or so before turning back to the store, she has the window down and can't get enough of the cool air, it feels so round, so satisfying.

After more cocaine and another drink they smoke like gamblers. June trades BOARDWALK to May who thinks she can't lose, and Kaslikoff puts hotels on all his cheap holdings and begins to rake in the play money.

Let's quit, June says, *I think we know who's going to win.*

No way, he tells them.

I'm tired.

Roll! he commands, with an intensity that makes the women uncomfortable.

He drains off the last of the scotch and finishes the coke. After June has sold all her properties to pay him, and he forces May to surrender the last railroad, he lets out an embarrassing victory cry and climbs up on the table scattering the game and shouting, *I'm the king of the fucking kitchen!* The table goes flying and he falls against a shelf which showers him with skillets and knives. He checks himself for protruding knife handles and then just lies there for a while, breathing.

In her room, June sits on the window ledge and stares across the lake. She lies down on the bed and listens to the white noise of her blood, feeling almost like herself.

Then the door opens and Kaslikoff comes in.

What are you doing?

I must have you, he says, climbing in beside her.

I don't love you.

Is that really what you want?

Can I tell you something?
Of course.
I didn't do it on purpose.
What?
It was only a silly mailbox.
You're fucking kidding, my car?

He runs down the stairs and June locks the door behind him.

Stepping onto the dock in the morning June radiates vibrations out across the lake. In the boathouse she finds a life jacket and two long white oars that she slides down from the rafters. A rowboat she found upside down on the dock she overturns onto the lake. Underneath it was a tackle box and a fishing rod ready to go. Kaslikoff didn't say which one of them died first but she hopes it was him; women have a talent for being left, a widow's gene, while men founder and come apart.

In the tackle box is a half-empty bottle of whisky; she takes it to the house for whoever wants it and has some breakfast of cold stew. May is wrapped in her sheet like a salad roll and Kaslikoff is unconscious on the floor behind the door.

The oars slip their locks a few times and June gets underway, pulling the lake in beneath her. Before Jerry was killed he had managed to separate from Betty,

June's mother. Even though it was his idea, he wasn't happy. The unforeseen consequences were that he lost contact with his daughter's daily life, with all her crazy friends. The apartment he rented in the West End was to his intellectual freedom what a nightmare is to loneliness. He wanted to go home but he couldn't accept the status quo, on a point of principle. Leaving his irrational wife was the rational thing to do. But he ended up with a depression he didn't know how to ignore, not even when June prepared the fish he brought back from trips she didn't accompany him on. Unusual things to amuse him, pike with Florentine sauce, curried bass with fiddleheads. She lit candles and toasted the old days while he scoffed at his broken heart.

She trolls an orange and black spoon for a while, then casts a fly and bobber near the shore and tries jigging a willow leaf for a spell. Maybe it was the time of year, or maybe the water was acidic. She doesn't remember Jerry ever mentioning this Lost Lake, and he knew them all.

Six

LEO PASSES THE phony twenties and lives off the principal for as long as it lasts. What's difficult to contemplate is stepping outside this cocoon of circumstance, where sentimentality degrades it all, to where only hatred rings true. He only wants the conflagration in his head to settle its score, the wrongness at his deepest intersections to be cut out. But it lurches on, his life, where luck is the centre attraction and you watch for as long as it lets you. If he can't make himself go back into people's garbage, what then?

He cruises the supermarket aisles with his last remnants of cold cash and stares at the deli slices laid out like expensive lingerie: black forest ham, lacy roast beef, translucent honey-cured heart, silky ox tongue. He runs an eye over the cheeses, quarter wheels and wedges.

He orders a roast beef with summer sausage and

Swiss on rye. The woman dressed in hospital whites lovingly cuts wide slabs of bread with a long curved blade, lays out all the delicate slices like a royal flush. If ever there was an intimate act . . .

Putting the sandwich on the baby seat of a cart, he travels the canned goods aisle, visits the cereal and baking needs. He ponders labels and squeezes apples while he savours each and every mouthful. He stops at the humorous greeting cards, then pushes the cart outside and around to the back of the building where he loads it with his tools and blankets and other things he's started to accumulate.

The greater portion of his days he spends searching for night shelter, though not necessarily sleep. He is often happy to crouch in a doorway like a streetlight painting of a man, with his head on his knees, listening to the echoes of the big bang.

Under the eaves of a concession stand along Spanish Banks he counts the grey ships in the bay, like pieces on a game board. He never sees them arrive and always misses their departures. Up to thirteen at a time, and never fewer than nine.

The moon outlines the sand as far out as the giant ships, their paper-thin reflections nearly touching the shore.

In the morning he finds a barge run aground. Late in the night it slipped anchor and thinking itself a wave came to play in the rocks. When the tide receded it was

a barge again, ominous as a lost building. Not willing
to be outdone, the sun appears. Leo slaps the side of its
hull, half expecting it to sound hollow. It smells of saw-
dust and scrap metal, and even though it's locked in
gravity Leo doesn't trust it. By evening three tugs are
in place, attached with their lines, waiting for the moon
to take up the slack, for the last anxious child to be
asleep.

Dusk is always so painstaking, placing its details just
so. The varnished pavement glimmers with gas station
flags. The temperature drops by exact increments.

One night he breaks into a public toilet. With his
hammer and screwdriver he makes short work of the
rotting wood around the bolt. Inside is dry but even
colder than outside, and the tiles echo the desolate
whispers of the water pipes.

Man isn't really adaptable, what he does is more of a
trick, something he's learned from rats, how to multiply
around garbage. He wonders how he could vanish, turn
off the projector and go home. His shopping cart is
looking at him, holding up its injured wheel.

He cruises restaurants for abandoned half-burgers
and settled Cokes, travels the back alleys of produce
stores, filling up on lettuce and remnants of steaks.
Interesting objects go in the cart, things he intends to
study when he has time. He finds a clock and winds it
up, creating a major personal crisis when he can't turn
the alarm off. A mandolin with no strings contained a

value impossible to calculate. When he finds a checker board with no checkers he trades the clock for a set in a junk store.

He surrenders his absurd pride. It makes no difference if he's the bum or somebody else. There has to be a bum, a mannequin for people to dress up with their moods. Places to shit are at a premium. More people indoors block his way with their packages and children.

On his way through a department store he stops to look at the shoes, at rack upon rack of garbage shipped in from countries where people didn't wear shoes. The cobbler's art was disappearing in the glint of some foreign eye.

In a second-hand clothing store he finds a decent pair of used work boots, with hard leather soles that are only one size too big. But there is nothing more pathetic looking than an old pair of shoes with the ghost of the previous owner still occupying them. Leo limps around the aisles, the soft tissue of his feet resisting the old impressions, bearing his weight at all the wrong spots. A thick pair of socks helps and he moves the price tag over to his old shoes. Conspicuous, like a man on stilts, he leaves the store in another man's gait.

Gunther laughs wildly and runs around the living room screaming. June puts her hands over her ears, tired of telling him to be quiet. He doesn't ever do what she tells him, and when she complains about this over the phone to her mother, the advice keeps coming. Why don't you try spanking him? Well, I can't because it's against the law, in case you haven't heard. Why don't you try talking to him? What works for me is reverse psychology. But there is nothing smarter than a child. Don't you know that? He'd reverse your reverse before you even opened your mouth. Why don't you take a course in childcare? Why don't you take a course in not being a jerk? You should read a book on anger management. Is it your intention to make me insane? Do you want to make me insane?

Eat up, Gunther, your dad'll be here soon.

When?

Soon.

How soon?

Soon soon.

Soon soon soon?

Soon soon soon soon soon.

June regrets getting him going again. He runs around singing the new one-word song. She gives up trying to get him to eat and scrapes his supper into the bag under the sink. A knock on the door brings him charging into the kitchen.

How's it going Gunner? His dad comes in full of insecure bluster. The sound of his voice makes June feel unstable.

Fine, says Gunther, grinning.

Is it going fine?

Yes, it's going fine, says the kid.

Is it going fine? his father asks again, not playfully.

Yes, Gunther replies, confused, his face becoming two faces, suspicious and excited.

Rick, in a dark two-piece, looks handsome and fit. When June met him she thought, finally a man as good looking as me. The hell her life has become must be payback for that astonishing vanity.

How's it going? he asks.

As though you care, she says, trying to shoot him down before he can tamper with her mind.

I care.

Yah?

Yeah. Me and that social worker you bagged, he says, smiling.

I thought you thought I was innocent.

Did I say you weren't?

She's out of her depth. *Get out of here before I attack you,* she says, playfully.

What do you think of that Gunner? Your mother is threatening me.

Go on, get out of here, she says, gently moving them towards the door.

Why don't you come with us? he asks.

What? Where?

We could all go out for something to eat. Have you eaten yet, Gunner?

No.

Come on, he says to June. *I'm buying.*

Forget it.

Gun', you want mummy to come with us, don't you?

She doesn't want to, Daddy.

Thank you darling, she says, kneeling down and kissing him.

You're just as gorgeous as ever, Rick says, using gorgeous like a misogynist word. He really doesn't know how dangerous he is. She gives Gunther another squeeze and zips up his jacket, tells him to be good.

Furniture oil, starch, mothballs, baths, and something deeper, old book smell, and the fragrance of churches. The hardwood floor gleams like amber where the congregation males move silent as ships in the night. The women are artful in heels, tapping resolutely on the sidewalk outside, and inside just as resolutely restrained. Weak light and bowed heads; stained glass animals graze in heaven. June has found her own church. Hers. None of these people know her mother.

A child bearing a golden cross leads a procession into the sanctuary: a choir of retired angels in ultramarine robes, followed by the minister, his female apprentice, and a beautiful black deacon.

The spunky, thinning minister plays a solemn character. He has radar for newcomers, shepherding them later to the coffee room for a chat, the young couples and single parents returning to the fold with their new-minted progeny to be stamped with Christian bafflement.

The minister's sermon is about divorce, the contradiction between the Bible and its meaning in our real lives. The suffering of Christ is the suffering of those among us who are remarried to divorced people. It's a perplexing topic, for everyone, especially for him, being twice divorced and finally truly in love.

The deacon, regal in her robes, asks the congregation to stand and sing Hymn Number 132 in the green book. *The lord shall keep us safe until he calls for us upon his mighty horn.* When it's over she gestures with her arms. The parishioners sit down, then kneel when she asks, stand up, sit down, and stand for another hymn. *The lord be with you,* she says. *And with you,* the congregation returns. As irritating and comforting as these rites are, they support and devastate her. She tugs at her clothes, rubs sleep from her eyes.

After the service, June goes to the coffee room and sits down at an empty table, looking around at the other people talking and gesturing, telling each other rumours and laughing. They all seem to have something June does not. She gets a cup of coffee and a plate of cookies and fidgets with her cup, looking at the large lipstick stain from her lips, thinking she should find a mirror.

An old woman in a motorized wheelchair comes by.

Do you mind if I park here?

Not at all.

Wasn't that a sermon for the record books? she asks when she's satisfied she can't get any closer to the table.

June smiles absently. She thought the sermon was all right.

Out of the mouths of babes, the old woman continues.

How long do your batteries last? June asks, admiring the chair, then regrets asking and says, *I'm sorry, that was a stupid question.*

Not at all, dear. I don't really know. I've never run out. A friend of mine went all the way downtown and back on hers.

Really?

You remind me of my daughter who lives in England.

England . . . June moans. *Don't talk to me about England.*

Bugger, the woman says, in an imitation Cockney accent, *you can't trust them bleedin' puddin' heads.* The old woman laughs wickedly.

I love your laugh, June says.

You're so kind.

Actually, I'm not. I'm a bit of a bitch.
You're no bitch.
How do you know?
At least not in an unpleasant way.
Can I get you a coffee?
I'd love a coffee, dear.

Her voice is like music, filled with uncanny tones. June watches her eat a cookie. Her tongue is clean and pink.

I haven't seen you here before, the old woman remarks.

I used to go to Saint Paul's.
It's a bit stuffy.
The minister's a nut.
What minister isn't?
What's the story with the gorgeous deacon?
Oh, you catch on fast.
I like this church. It seems so friendly.
Well, good then, I can expect to see you here next week?

Next Sunday June looks for her new friend, and she's easy to spot, her chair double-parked at the end of the last row. She waves at June and indicates the pew beside her, moving her coat from the seat.

I'm Tess, by the way, she says, taking June's hand.
June, says June.

That's a lovely name.

The apprentice minister is a Caucasian woman around the same age as the minister. She's doing the sermon this Sunday and prefaces it with some personal background about her education, being a linguist as well as a biblical scholar. She talks about the story of Jezebel from the Book of Revelations, having read it in the original Aramaic. She explains the original meaning of the word "fornication," which meant "turning one's back on God." Explaining as well that a Jezebel was someone who had given up prayer, trying to usurp the power of God by not listening to the true voice in her heart.

She doesn't know the meaning of fornicate, says Tess. *I know fornicate.*

The apprentice pleads with the congregation to look at their own lives, to discover what, or who, for them personally, is the Jezebel of their heart.

I can think of a few men who could turn her away from God, Tess smirks.

After the service, they file past the minister and his minions, the deacon on one side of him and his apprentice on the other. They are standing outside the coffee room, trying to shake hands with everyone.

So, June, tell me, what do you do?

I'm a single mom.

Oh, how tragic, Tess says, *talented woman like you.*

It's not that bad, June says defensively. *What am I saying, of course it is.*

From beyond the bottleneck come the inviting smells of pastry and coffee.

I could have been a single mom, Tess says. Who wants to raise a child with a man around? Not that I have anything against men, mind you, but everything in its place. In the bed and under the hood. If you don't mind my saying. My God, I'm going to scare you away. What else do you do? I mean, are you a composer, an author, a sculptress? I myself am an author. I have six books of poetry planned.

I thought you said you had a daughter.

Well, yes, actually the daughter of a man I once knew. He died of something undignified and she stayed with me until she finished high school. I didn't like it, but what was I going to do, send her out to be eaten by her own kind? Aren't we an appalling species?

I'm in the market.

For?

Penny stocks.

That takes guts.

The lifestyle can kill you. The people you meet.

You mean the men. Dogs will always sniff you out. I used to dress like a plumber to hide my figure. I have the perfect disguise now. I'm an old lady, a crippled one. It takes a rare breed to see through all this.

The courthouse gleams in the sun, like a terrarium, all

glass. The business towers around it seem to lean in, to tell tasteless jokes. Everywhere are boy lawyers in slit throat neckties. Running up the steps June has to stop and catch her breath. Her heart doesn't so much beat as wag like a branch in a flood. Behind her the city rolls and knocks, a steady thrum from the subbasement of hell. She's exhausted and the day has hardly begun. She rubs her eyes and brain cells detonate. Justice is damaging her, the terror of watching it emerge so slowly from its hole, all mumbo-jumbo, hissing neutrality. Sleepless nights she rewrites the days: what she should have said or might have done, but she couldn't focus on the process and she has stumbled at every turn. If she could just relax, if they'd let her take something.

Enny is waiting for her inside the main entrance. She guides her through the crossword puzzle common areas, where several storeys overhead sunlight strains through the greenhouse ceiling. There are birds, too, but June can't tell which side they're on.

She finds a reflection in a glass case and puts on her glasses. They make her look more intelligent. She tells herself she has nothing to worry about; she has socialized with judges and philosophers, held them in scrotum-tingling thrall with stories of overnight fortunes.

We have a solid case, Enny tells her. *Stop worrying. The boat is in the river. It's going where it's going.*

A case based on something she calls "extreme duress." Which sounds to June pretty much like an admission of guilt, the stressed-out cousin to a plea of insanity.

All we can do is throw our coins in the fountain.

What do you think the best way is to control prison guards? June wonders out loud, as she reapplies her lipstick, irritating Enny.

For God's sake, stop putting lipstick on, she snaps.

Enny says she needs some air and heads outside for a smoke, a habit she thought she'd given up.

June paces around trying to stay calm. So much depends on the judge, is what they say. It's what she thinks about day and night. That it comes down to some jerk's opinion. And that's what preys on her mind. She knows she doesn't come off well in translation. And when Enny heard which judge got their case her face drew a short straw. She said that at least he follows the book and he's fair. Since when did fairness become a consolation prize?

June is enthralled with the idea of incarceration. To be taken away from Rick and Jean and the good intentions falling all over themselves to tell her how good she is, even when she's not; and once their foot is in the door, how bad she is at everything. The supervisors, police officers, clerks, receptionists and so-called friends. It's a gang rape. As if God gives a fuck what any of them think. How bad could it be? Throw away the key.

Enny returns with a guilty cigarette smell, and then a clerk appears to tell them which door to go through. It must be a holding area, June thinks, taking the chair Enny holds out for her. It's an ordinary conference room with ceiling tiles and cement walls. Lime Green is there with about ten supporters, wearing an impressive neck brace, and her hair looks different, ordinary, mousy brown.

The judge enters like an actor with a headache and takes the biggest chair, the one with arm rests, at a table like the one June and Enny have and the one the prosecutor has, who's sitting there by himself, pushing his glasses up on his nose.

Lime Green is sitting with her supporters in the row of chairs against the back wall. She's there as a spectator, she's not even involved. It's June against everyone. Her crime was apparently not against a person but against society as a whole, against humanity. If she had something sharp in her hands she'd manufacture some justice.

The judge's dull red eyes are on her, as though reading her thoughts. But June is one up on him, she can see his soul, that there's something chewing on it, a mistress, or a habit.

The prosecutor is poised, efficient, like Enny, a reasonably good dancer. But the judge has no time for rookies and rhetoric. It's an open and shut case. June assaulted a woman, an officer of the court, a public servant no less, and no amount of provocation could have justified it. He sentences her to one-year's probation and one hundred hours of community service.

Enny is surprised and not surprised, but she spins the verdict as a triumph.

A year's probation and community service, she says, nodding her head optimistically.

June steps off the bus on the south side of Broadway, at Main. Being strictly a westside girl, she's wary of East Van, with its pioneers and wasted storefronts. She stands on the corner waiting for the light, while other pedestrians ignore the red hand, betting it all on some stranger behind tinted glass. When the signal changes, June is still blocked by buses crowding the crosswalk on the other side. The light changes back to red and she is embarrassed to be the only fool standing in the crosswalk, so she looks for a break in the traffic and runs.

She makes for the entrance of the seven-floor brownstone on the corner, pushing through the human meat, a new criminal record giving her license, compliments of the ministry. It's a new nationality for her, an exclusive club, according her all the rights and privileges therein.

When their little enterprise failed, May took a job with a firm that was trying to rebuild after the crash.

Relocated at the intersection of three major arteries, the building and its gigantic roof sign can be seen from all over the city. Up close it's imposing and shabby; that is, if you haven't already looked away. Inside, the doors have old-fashioned knobs and rattling glass. There is a discernible lack of air conditioning.

May's fifth-floor window is open and the fans are going, a wasted one on the ceiling and an industrial rotator that convulses her over-watered plants and flutters the papers weighted to her desk. When they put the building up, natural light hadn't been invented, though there is something suitable and funereal about the dimness.

May is on the phone and waves June towards a chair. May wasn't great looking to begin with but now something is weighing on her, making her seem ancient and hard. June goes to the window and leans out. There's a ledge that would be just wide enough to crawl out on. Built during the great depression, the building understands the loser better than the loser understands herself. Below on the street a trolley bus flounders, sparks fly, and its arms go flailing. The driver climbs down and walks casually around and behind the bus and out into traffic. An old man in a walker takes the opportunity to cross the intersection diagonally, and a barber in a white shirt leans on a cigarette and watches his progress. It's an area for small presses and pool halls, the city's tattooed bone sticking out of its flesh. To be who you are and accept it, there was something in that.

Has anyone ever been electrocuted by a bus? June wonders.

I saw an old woman get hit by a truck, May says.

I mean, how safe can that be? referring to the bus driver.

There was a pool of blood on the road.

Did you hear Walsh died? June asks, remembering why she's there.

You have no idea how much of it there is, May continues morbidly.

He died of natural causes, that's the amazing part. It was the gentlemanly thing to do. Everyone can stop being embarrassed now.

Good timing, it shows class.

It was the largest stock fraud in history. When it came to its inevitable conclusion, exploration stocks everywhere went through the floor. Even though Bre-X wasn't listed on the VSE, Vancouver's already salty reputation took another beating, as a matter of form. It was pure Wild West. The stock had climbed from a few cents to hundreds of dollars, but it turned into a doomsday comet for some very prominent people, Kaslikoff amongst them. A pall fell over the western exchanges, with their prospectors and empty shells with little more in the assets column than an iffy claim and a Piper Cub.

A good promoter can sell anything: hair regeneration tonics, cures for blindness, or turn a snowball's chance in hell into General Dynamics. A good promoter is one in a million and that was Walsh. Now Walsh is dead.

Every bar on Howe Street was having a wake for the man. At The Bull June and May find what they're looking for, cocaine and whisky. Kaslikoff pulls out a couple of chairs and waves them over.

June watches the here-and-now come into sharp focus. Listening to her friends' brassy voices, she wonders how they can laugh so much. Three conversations are going at once, and underneath it all is the subtext of drinks: the salutation, the questioning rattle, innuendo in a spill.

Kaslikoff has lost before and fought his way back to lose it all again. The Prince of Howe Street is what some of his friends call him, because he advised them to get out of Bre-X. Fortunes were rescued and children were being named after him. It was a mystery to everyone why, at the last minute, he got back in, buying up shares at a fortieth their former value, betting everything on the final damning independent assay, whose release ended all speculation.

He drapes a heavy arm over June's shoulder.

The quicker you learn that money doesn't matter, the quicker you'll have more than you need, he tells her.

His rough looks are softened by a vacant expression. He drinks double scotches that don't touch him.

How can you have too much? asks one of the men. *I mean, come on.*

Kaslikoff gives him a grieved expression: *Believe me, Tony, you don't really want to know.*

Why did you stay in when you told us to get out?

Everyone at the table wants to hear his answer.

I don't know, he says.

You said it was too good to be true.

It was too good to be true.

Why didn't you stay out?

He turns his glass on the table, like a dial, indicating something only June picks up on.

I can't understand you, May badgers.

Who here likes GBP? June asks, trying to change the subject.

I'm thinking of getting into blue chips, Tony says.

We're penny stock players, always will be, says Kaslikoff. *There's no more fortunes to be made on Microsoft.*

Be safe, buy up American dollars, May says.

One nuke and they're on their knees, says Kaslikoff, *two and their economy vanishes like a thief in the night. And where do you think that leaves us?*

What about diamonds in the north? June asks.

Diamonds belong on your finger, Kaslikoff says. He takes her hand and kisses it. *When are you going to marry me, June?*

The other men at the table laugh.

You should take me more seriously. I've got a criminal record, she says.

Let me rephrase that then. Murder me my beloved, kill me dead.

I want an emerald.

How big?

As big as your head.

Which one?

June can't figure out what May sees in him, and it's beginning to look like May can't figure it out either. The three of them decide to go back to his place for a nightcap. He calls a cab and tells the young driver to take the long way around the park.

Cruising in under the pedestrian overpass, the forest looms up on their left, with the city jogging into view on the right, reflecting in the harbour. There is an emotion specific to the park, a kind of love, a suspension of anxieties accompanying the familiar smells. They roll past the scuba diver on the rock that everyone thinks is a mermaid. June sees Jerry's ghost out there on his sea legs, filling up at the marine Chevron station.

The bridge is outlined in pale white lights, inadequate cover for an old woman, a skirt she holds up as she wades in. She means everything to the city, though resented and taken advantage of.

Kaslikoff asks the driver to pull over, where they all get out. He talks the driver into coming along and they file out on the narrow sidewalk where the traffic beats the air beside them. They lean over the railing and stare down at the hard shadows. A tall ship is passing underneath, the lights of its mast a long way down.

Isn't this great? Kaslikoff says. *This is one of my favourite places.*

He climbs over the rail and into the superstructure, agile and in his element, apparently.

What are you doing? May complains.

Come on you two. It really clears the mind. I feel marvellous.

You'll fall.

I should be so lucky.

Your friend is nuts, says the driver.

Kaslikoff climbs around on the girders.

Look, I'm the human fly.

This is stupid. You're scaring us.

Come on, May, try it. How about you, June? You like new experiences, don't you?

You say it'll clear my head?

Come on then.

She climbs over the fence onto a maintenance gangway. She is terrified but keeps going, inching her way to the edge. Holding a beam she leans out and looks down. She feels her fear turn into a rush, inflated and magnificent. Embracing the beam she feels the rapture of the bridge, as it embraces her back.

If you fall, who's going to pay me? shouts the driver,

taking May's side, afraid for himself, that he's a part of this.

Why are so many old people crazy? he asks May.

May looks at him and studies his young face, the naïveté.

Driver. Don't you want to come out here? Kaslikoff shouts.

Come on back in, sir.

Okay, you're right, give me a hand.

The driver reaches for him over the side, taking hold of his lapels, but then Kaslikoff leans back and holds his arms up, putting his life in the bewildered driver's fingers.

Have you got me? he laughs. *You wouldn't let go, would you driver?*

Kaslikoff, what are you doing? June can't help laughing.

Please, you're heavy, the driver says.

No, I'm light as a bird, Kaslikoff cries.

June feels sorry for May, involved with someone so blatantly abnormal. She feels the familiar trance coming to cover her, to bury her, where nothing hurts and nothing feels good, where she's spent most of her life, the prison of *I can't,* though *I won't* was more to the point, and it's too late to change anything. She can hear the laughing, May and Kaslikoff and the driver now as well. It makes her feel empty because it's never her laughter. Holding the beam in one hand she stands closer to the edge, looking around at the cold city, where choice passed for freedom, and equality was a form of brainwashing, a place ruled by the expectations of the dead. What good was it when you felt like shit all the time? A strange feeling takes her fear away, like hooking a big one that runs with your line before you can tighten the drag. She releases her fingers and her identity dissolves in the night sky and the moment of falling. But no, it's Kaslikoff, and he's hurting her wrist. She's crying and he's looking at her with no judgement, no hurt or surprise, only an understanding, a knowledge of where that moment is.

Seven

L EO HAS FOUND a clean bed, though it's in a dormi-
tory full of stillborn husbands and aged children.
He lies awake listening to their pitiful waves sucking at
an empty shore: useless men shrouded in bigotry and
clawing at their coffin latches. A bitter loyalty exists
between them. It was the material they built their
houses on, the shifting mass that swallowed them without a trace. It was their only subject, in a language with
fifty-seven names for hatred. It was their only emotion,
the glue that held them together apart. Integrity was
demonstrated by a lack of integrity, absence was mis-
taken for intimacy. Hatred mistakes love for death and
must defend against it with all it has.

It's different for a woman, Leo thinks. A woman
can be somebody's mother, or a wife, or a tomboy.
While a man is just a man, no matter what you chop
or who plumbs your soul. He puts his hand inside his

shirt and feels the animal fur. A woman folds inward, waiting for the voice that ploughs her under and brings water. But a man is newborn day after terrifying day. He must venture beyond his own skin to scavenge for his luck. He is ruthless because he must be, because someone is waiting for him to return. Every father is a fallen angel whose principal preoccupation is in hiding that fact.

Leo keeps his tool belt close, curled like a sleeping cat under his cot. His tools are his road back to the somewhere of his old self, a place constructed of memories and ideas and furnished with hope and time. They are admirable, dense and specific; even battered and tarnished their usefulness is reduced by nothing, their hammerness, their plierness. How well they understand the intimacies of wood. Their respect for the flesh that held them not absolute, showing their hand if Leo got irreverent or impatient.

Institutional mornings are a trial. It exhausts him to hide his rage, to look benignly past the other men to the spaces between, while eating a breakfast of hard-boiled eggs. He makes up his mind to return to the street.

Pushing his cart down the boardwalk onto Granville Island, the bridge hangs overhead in his peripheral vision and the traffic congests underneath. They come for the blessing of a parking space and the game of chance. The wheel of his shopping cart is completely seized up, conspicuous and noisy, and people turn away before they see their reflection on him.

Cars entering turn right while the bridge carries on over top the island, sheltering the jungley corridors of fishing reel museums and blown glass boutiques, the frame timber warehouses gutted for parking spaces.

In the market, fruit will fall into his pockets and lost lunches will beg to be rescued. The feeling of enclosure is in persistent abeyance with movement, catching the eye: the hourglass of a woman, a flock of pigeons fanning out. The bridge is too high to be sufficient cover and rain comes in on wind shavings, peeling off its reverse cantilever structure like an arbor flowing white roses.

The Cambie Street Bridge was poured somewhere far away and shipped to the site in sections. With few places underneath to take shelter, Leo is forced to detour away from the lay of the land, around what remains of downtown's heavy industry and along past the city engineer's pyramids of winter sand. Twisting back to the shore across from Science World, the path widens into a cobblestone promenade built out over the rising and falling tide.

Investigating a hunch, he finds a hole in the fence and goes down the bank and finds himself looking up at the underside of the promenade. The piles and beams are coated in creosote, and he crawls under and along the abutment that anchors it to the shore and kneels in the soft sand.

He stares at the polished water until he's almost asleep, listening to the sound of water in the rocks against the shore, sounding vaguely sexual. Without a woman to put it in its place, what was the world? A memory of a desire. Surfaces without texture. He idolized his mother and imagined himself like her. When he was old enough to be left alone he lived in her closet.

He opens his eyes and another man is crouching in the opening.

Hey shithead, says a weak and leathery voice.

What?

Shit, man . . . beat it!

There's lots of room.

Like shit there is. Scram. Move on.

I just got comfortable.

Shit . . . wait 'til Big Mike gets here. He killed a man.

I've killed two or three.

Shit . . .

The small, emaciated man crawls past him into the gloom at the other end of the enclosure.

Leo worms his impression a little deeper into the sand, hoping this Big Mike is a ploy or a figment of the little guy's imagination.

That your shit in the cart? he hears, a larger voice, a man on his haunches blocks the sky.

Yah?

I want those blankets.

I have an extra blanket I can let you have.

Big Mike bends into the shadow, *What else you got?*

Checkers.

All the pieces there?

Yah, most.

I get sick of you, you're gone.

If you don't kill him first, eh, Mike?

Shut up, turd.

Leo gets his things from the cart and hides his tool belt in a crevice between the deck and the bank. He hands a blanket to Big Mike and the checkers to the little guy, the little Mike. Leo keeps his distance while the Mikes get a small fire going in an attempt to shed some light on the game.

I feel like shit, says Little Mike. *I don't feel like shit, man,* he reiterates, when Big Mike doesn't respond.

Shut up . . .

I wanna drink.

Big Mike pulls a bottle out of his bag and waves it in Little Mike's face, teasing him, then offers it to Leo. The mechanics of self-destruction once begun must run their course, like all contraptions, with their balls and gutters, their incessant movement, always down, bottom being the great attractor. Contradict it any way you like, but you've been spoken for. Suffering is such an intimate act, how can you not love it back?

He shifts closer to the fire and takes a mouthful, then hands it to Little Mike. When Big Mike offers him another, Leo turns it down.

You sure, man?

Yah, I shouldn't touch the shit, he says. Did drinking really destroy his mother? Does addiction have that kind of power? Did it necessarily shift you to that other orbit, the one for which no counterbalance exists?

It's good shit.

No shit, man. I can't, he says, though he longs to.

She lived in her mind and could therefore never make good choices. She never finished what she began, and every victory was tainted with compromise and broken promises.

You shittin' me? asks Big Mike.

I shit you not. I'm a real head case.

What a shithead, eh? Big Mike says, elbowing his confused friend.

A guy who chooses not to drink, Big Mike explains, *is a prissy dork, but a guy who doesn't drink 'cause he turns into Hitler is a fucking hero.*

Leo can't tell if he's being praised or ridiculed.

I'm not sure the analogy is apt, but . . .

I mean it. If I had a hat I'd take it off to you.

Shit heil! barks Little Mike, apparently agreeing.

Forgiveness, that's the thing, right? says Big Mike, *You hear it all the time, turn the outer cheek.*

Leo looks more closely at the man in the flickering light.

If I can scare up some shit to eat at Granville Island, Leo says, *I'll share it with you bastards.*

To contain his mother's darkness became Leo's secret talent. If she got too happy, he reined her in. When she got depressed, he kept her from collapsing.

Shit man . . . Chinatown's just right here, says Big Mike.

Chinatown? No . . .

Even this, his homelessness, Leo's somehow managed to contain. With False Creek standing between him and downtown, by not crossing over the bridges, meant he was going to be okay, that he would find the road back. Raising his son was a process of limits placed on enthusiasm. His wife managed to keep within his expectations for as long as it lasted. He kept himself in a jar with holes punched in the lid and considered himself a free man. But he's tricked himself after all by coming this far east, to where the inlet ends, where there are no barrier bridges. Just one block and he's in Chinatown, with one more to skid row.

The drink Big Mike gave him has got his blood rolling. It's an automatic thing, his heart, like a headless chicken; it keeps its secrets and runs into walls. Hastings Street was a fascinating place to see from the window of a bus, or enclosed in the safety zone of a girlfriend. There were safe ways for a man to explore his worst fears. It was a cathartic experience to see the Chinese medicine emporiums with the appalling hotels wedged in between, the moderately rich and the entirely poor on top of each other like ghosts. But drifting through on foot Leo sees the monster of here and now and he wishes he'd taken another drink.

He keeps his head down, trying to relax. Empty is the right and just state of a man's ambition. Run it up the flagpole and print it on your money. The heartless and the deluded, the poor and the destitute. Ex-kings and reincarnations of Judy Garland are everywhere and Leo moves among them, filling his pockets with weird tubers and Chinese candies in strange wrappings.

There are no sirens in a city of the deaf, but suddenly many of them converge from every direction and their overwhelming charisma draws him towards a column of smoke rising up from Science World.

Fire trucks and patrol cars have surrounded the promenade and thick black curtains billow up from the two open sides. Police manning the barricades are turning away the moths and the baby moths with bright backpacks as Leo comes running up, shouting, *What about my tools?*

A fireboat is trying to direct an arc of water under the deck while two trucks on top are doing their best, but they can't touch the flames either. Leo runs past the barriers and around the trucks and cuts through a hole in the fence. Voices are shouting at him to stop. Flames have broken through the sidewalk and the firemen direct their cannons at the opening. Leo pulls his jacket over his head and claws his way forward.

There is more gum stuck to the pavement down here, June notices. It smells of broken transmissions and rotting vegetables. Mysterious doors on the sides of buildings hold cryptic signs: Stormy Petrels, SA. The Downtown Eastside is a honeycomb of old buildings, a hatchery of anonymous enterprise, and everywhere is a palpable . . . something. At the Mission, men are waiting to get in, some are standing, some sitting on the steps, elbows on their knees, cigarette smoke curling from battered fingers.

Inside, June stands out of the way, waiting for the coordinator to tell her what to do. There are five women in the kitchen and any number cleaning up, serving, catering to the hundred and fifty or so men, women, and children merged in the common denominator of failure, which apparently includes those serving them, which puts June where on the scale of things? She prefers the kitchen, where she at least has some control, where it's relatively predictable. Doing the dishes makes the hours cycle through faster. The rubber gloves have created patches of eczema on her hands, and her wrists are sore from the heavy pans; she's cut herself on knives people stupidly load edge up in the racks. In the mess she has to stay alert, duck when personalities start to multiply.

The volunteer bureau had other things she could do, from teaching classes to visiting old people. But there is nothing she knows well enough to teach, except for maybe the market, and she wouldn't wish it on her worst enemy. She can't remember the last time she picked a winner. And most old people scare her, with their hardwood canes and motorized hearts. What if she broke one, pushed the wrong button? The woman at the bureau was persistent, saying the Mission was desperate. She should have held out for something easier. There is nothing pleasing about this work, nothing hobby. She returns home stressed to the snapping point and in need of a bath. She didn't come into it with illusions; but even so, reality is always so . . . below average.

She pushes a cauldron of thick soup on a service cart and ladles it into bowls on long tables. She silently hands out pieces of pre-buttered white bread and is supposed to ask them first if they want it, but they always say yes, and sometimes she doesn't have the self-confidence to open her mouth. She doesn't want them to hear her brittle voice, to crumble it into their soup. She cuts cake and readies cups for coffee or tea.

Another choice, which seems ridiculous. If you told them there was only coffee, you wouldn't hear any complaints. Tea drinkers hum and haw, verge on theatre of the absurd, ask for ridiculous wedges of lemon, dollops of cream.

When the meal is over she runs the cart between tables to gather the bone and blood. She makes separate piles of plates and glasses and mugs beside the sink, and the utensils go into a shallow plastic tray. The woman doing the rinsing and loading rarely speaks and doesn't like to listen, neutrality being a gesture of familiarity for her. Four hours exhaust June like twelve. Sweaty and sticky, she ends her shift in the bathroom. In the harsh light she looks utterly hopeless.

The men mill around in the warm evening air, smoking, some huddled in conversation, while others keep their distance, afraid to be part of anything, but hesitant to go back out there. Is the fact that they're bums part of their awareness? Do they know? Or do they breathe a fine mist of denial, believe they are masters of their universe, like every man? Walking to the bus stop she wonders why the pavement has to smell like garbage.

Eight

THE GLASS DOORS of International Arrivals slide open and the passengers from several flights come streaming through all in a pointless hurry, having flown an entire ocean to come to this, a standstill at the baggage carousel. June sees her mother in the middle of the crowd, comfortable with being neither first nor last, nervously looking around for the daughter she's sure has forgotten her. As old-fashioned as ever, with her hats and handbags and short-sleeved dresses. Even her name bothered June; "Beth" or "Elizabeth" or "Liz," any of which would have been tolerable. But no, it had to be Betty, which sounded fine on a British tongue, but Canadians made it sound like Behy or Beddy, which made June's skin crawl. Her attention is arrested by the empty luggage belt descending from the ceiling—as though this was what the human race was all about, through the tectonic movement of the centuries, and the wars to end war.

Finally suitcases begin to appear, four of them, and then nothing. June smirks. The workers on the floor above must be distracted, probably admiring each other's polyester-cotton blend navy coveralls. June was watching them earlier riding around on little tractors, pulling little trains, crashing through the No Admittance doors. Betty is beginning to ask stupid questions of the people around her, as if she was the only one in the dark. *Do you suppose something has happened? They aren't on strike are they?*

June can't take it any more. The old woman is beginning to embarrass her.

Hi, she says, wedging in beside her.

Where have you been? Betty asks, sounding relieved and perturbed.

Right here.

Didn't you see me come down?

Of course I did.

Why did you leave me standing here?

I didn't. I'm here.

I've been standing here for fifteen minutes.

More like five. Is that your bag? June asks, trying to distract her.

No . . . I have the same bags I've always had. You know what they look like. The blue one with the wheels and the brown one with the broken strap.

June falls in with the group, waiting for the luggage, watching the empty conveyer like a convention of would-be telepaths.

Run and get a cart, would you dear, Betty says.

They're all taken, she tells her.

How could they be? Go have a look, at least.

I can see from here.

I can't see past all these . . . people.

People aren't really people to Betty. They are animals in people suits. Betty is alone in the world. Even her friends aren't people. They don't have her understanding of religious ideals, or human nature. They don't have her sense of fair play, her sense of nobility, her ability to raise children. They aren't widows in the same way she is, because they don't understand the dead like she does. The dead know their place.

If you're not going to find a cart, I will, says Betty, leaving June to watch for the bags. June doesn't know why she gets pleasure from her mother's distress. She could just as easily be nice. But then Betty would have total control and June knows what that leaves for her. Luggage starts to appear again and June steps forward to claim her mother's bags. She drags them over near the exit and goes to find Betty.

She's easy to spot, Queen Elizabeth's cranky dark twin, in her horrible dress. She's halfway across the terminal struggling with a cart that has its own idea about where it's going.

I have your bags, June tells her.
Here, you push this thing.
We don't need it.
You left my things untended?
They'll be fine.
How could you do that?
No one's going to steal your clothes.
Take the cart.
We don't need it.
Take it!

June and Gunther moved into Leo's old basement suite for the cheaper rent, but it's so small and hard to make look decent. It's really impossible with toys everywhere and her crappy furniture. Betty can barely summon the strength to walk into it. June puts her things in the bedroom, which she did try to fix up for her. Betty lies down for half an hour before she emerges in a housecoat and asks for a glass of water. It's late but they sit up for a cup of tea. Betty tries to get comfortable on the broken sofa and stares at the stains on the carpet.

What's that? she asks.
Paint.
What kind of paint?
What does it matter what kind of paint? Paint.
He plays with his paints on the carpet?
When he has no place else.

Betty starts to slur her words and, saying a morose goodnight, pushes herself off to bed. June sleeps in the living room on Gunther's foam, which smells of pee and doesn't give her much support.

In the morning, sleep and gravity have overthrown Betty's optimism, what there was of it. She eats the breakfast June prepares, bacon and poached eggs on toast. There's no part of her face that isn't wrinkled or sagging. When she was young she was pretty, prettier than June at the same age, something June doesn't like thinking about. She doesn't know how she'll stand it, being ugly.

Didn't Oregon legalize euthanasia? June asks.

Why do you ask me that?

It's in the news lately. It makes you think. How much do you think it would cost?

You want rid of me that bad? England's not far enough for you?

I didn't mean for you, for christ's sake mother, sometimes you just don't listen.

I suppose there's some truth in that, she admits.

There's a knock on the door and then Gunther arrives like a terrorist's blast, followed by his uncomfortable father. *Gramma,* he screams, and throws himself at her.

Rick asks her about the flight and she tells him about it, going into unnecessary detail as a way to cope with the child.

So the ceremony is tomorrow? Rick says.

Yes, tomorrow.

It's such a good idea, the bench.

It was actually June's idea.

It wasn't my idea, June says from the kitchen.

She found a lovely spot overlooking English Bay. You are coming to the ceremony, I hope?

I hadn't actually been invited. I'm not sure June wants me there.

He's right, she doesn't want him there. She doesn't want him anywhere. She doesn't want him in her apartment right now. She doesn't want to have to think about him or plan around him or be stood up by him or play down to him. He doesn't belong and here was Betty belonging him. June puts a hold on her anger. It would only make matters worse. She doesn't know how, but it would unite them against her.

It's all right if Rick comes tomorrow, isn't it dear?

Of course.

Betty's a pushover for a handsome face and a reassuring voice. Rick keeps calling Gunther to his side, using him to locate himself, and as a conversation piece. It's almost like he's taken charge of the kid to let June off the hook for a while. What a husband might do, one who cared, one who paid attention to things.

When the city crew was putting up the memorial bench June went to Vanier Park a few times to check on their progress. One day there was a rectangle cut out of

the grass, another day the cement was being poured.
The workmen seemed to exist in another dimension, a
slower, happier one. It was beautiful weather and even
the simplest things seemed to give them pleasure, like
the weight of a shovel handle on their shoulders, the
curiosity of a woman watching them.

Betty left the inscription up to June. Another surprise. She used Gunther's watercolours to draw the
letters in a rough script. "In Loving Memory" was
too tombstone. This was a bench, overlooking the
unfortunately named English Bay. "Rest in God."
"Bridge Over Troubled Waters." "Missed By His
Friends." Nothing sounded right. She forgot about it
for a while until someone from the parks board called
and she had to decide. "Gone fishin'," she said to the
woman on the phone. It just popped into her head.

It was for the twentieth anniversary of Jerry's death.
The idea of the memorial took Jerry's buddies by surprise, the ones June could locate. Four of them show
up and mill about, taking in the view, trying out the
new bench and flirting with June. Guys she has known
her whole life, back when they were less grey and more
dangerous. One of them brought a bottle of Baby
Duck and some plastic glasses.

Why are you doing this now? asks Jerry's best
friend Ted.

Betty's guilt finally got the better of her, June answers.
Guilt for what?

For taking Jerry back to England.
You mean his ashes?
He hated England.

They reminisce about Jerry's battered pickup truck and remember how handsome he was, a quality they miss when looking at some bad pictures of him. Point a camera at him and he involuntarily put on the mug. June had tried to catch him off-guard, to capture his real dimensions, but rarely succeeded. She tells them she still keeps his fishing reel in the junk drawer and that she still has dreams about him.

A minister from the local Anglican Church reads a few passages chosen by Betty. They bow their heads in a pose unfamiliar to most of them and when June looks up she sees Rick's car pulling into the parking lot. Betty is put out with him for being late and when Gunther goes looking for her he finds her cold. Rick tries to horn in on the conversation June is having with the men but she sends him away, and he ends up sitting on the bench with his son between him and Betty, staring at the bay.

Gunther gets chilled and snuggles himself unconsciously into the folds of her coat, scooping up the warmth from her body. She looks at him with a reluctant loving smile and puts an arm around him.

The next day Betty and June march around The Bay, taking the escalator from floor to floor, aimlessly looking at furniture.

How do you like that one? Betty is referring to a paisley brocade wing-back sofa.

June shakes her head.

What about this one?

Leather? You're kidding.

You don't like leather?

Of course I like leather. In an office or a car, not in a house. Mars calling mother.

You pick one.

I kind of like this one.

It's plain.

It's tasteful.

A man in a two-piece suit strides over smelling of cigarette smoke.

Can I help you? he asks.

Yes, says Betty, *we'll take this one, the tasteful plain one.*

Mother, June laughs, thinking it's a joke.

Anything else? the clerk inquires.

A rug. A nice, tasteful plain one, to go with the sofa.

What are you doing?

They follow him through the labyrinth of newness. Betty knows exactly what she's doing. June follows, shaking her head. She should refuse expensive gifts, shouldn't she? Isn't there an unwritten law about taking things from your parents, lest they treat you like a child and control you 'til the grave—theirs or, more likely, yours. But how can she refuse? And how does she thank her without embarrassing them both?

In the rug department Betty goes for a wine and beige oriental pattern and is surprised when June likes it too.

Why are you doing this?

I simply am.

And one last thing, Betty says to the salesman. *A table. A small table for a child to paint on.*

When they're on the bus going home Betty puts a hand on June's knee.

Thank you for letting me do that, she says.

There is tenderness in her voice. June touches her arm and gives it a little squeeze.

You're welcome, she says.

Rick cleaned up his car and volunteered to drive Betty to the airport. He replaced the old coat hanger antenna with a new coat hanger and hung an air freshener from the mirror. For some reason Rick respects Betty. She was judgemental, sure, but he thought that was the point. What he didn't live up to made him who he was. And now he's trying to prove something, and driving like a senile chauffeur.

Rick, that pine tree thing is overwhelming, says June.

Thanks.

I mean it stinks.

Gunther, gunner, do you like daddy's ornament?

Uh huh.

Betty shakes her head. She's never seen anything

like it. Most people are just bad parents, though parents are what they are. This one abdicates the role. He's made his son his master. She feels sorry for the whole lot of them, the generation of lost knowledge. Most probably can't even wind a clock. For the boy to survive he will have to reinvent a world he understands out of this mess. Where did they come up with Gunther as a name anyway? It sounds German, which neither of them are. Probably from a cartoon character or something. You name pets that way, not children, unless you're training them to slit your throat in your sleep. Betty goes into her purse to find a Valium.

At the airport, Rick and Gunther say their good-byes to Betty at the curb. Rick manages to hold onto his aplomb for a while longer. He graciously bows while jingling his keys in his pocket. Gunther stretches his arms up to Betty and gets a face full of kisses, which makes him glisten. June goes into the terminal with her.

That Rick has certainly changed, Betty says. *He seems almost charming.*

You never were a good judge of character.

He sure seems to be interested in you again.

That's what makes me nervous.

I'd feel better about you staying in this country if I knew you were settled.

Settled?

I should have had you in England.

Mother, you're being delusional.

People shouldn't be alone. That just doesn't work.

Betty embraces her and kisses her lips and June gets a feeling like she's missing something. Something doesn't add up. Like there's another hand at work here. She wonders, does Betty have a man? They embrace and Betty goes through a barrier where June can't follow. That would explain her generosity, and that little ironic smile June's been noticing.

Mother, June calls out, *are you getting laid?*

Betty stands there, bodies flowing around her.

Why didn't you tell me you had a boyfriend?

You were so attached to your father, I . . .

Mother!

Betty gets caught up in the movement of people and from the last security gate she waves. June waves back, but Betty's already gone.

Leo's bed is a living thing. Air in the mattress makes rustling sounds as gently under him it shifts, like a hand, the Fifty Foot Woman from the old movie, her fingers thoughtfully, lovingly caressing him. Her image was the first thing to awaken Leo's machinery of desire. As a boy he stared at the flickering beauty, barely covered in the rags of her former human size, as she rampaged through town, unstoppable by armies or by reason, least of all by reason. Leo's supper is on a gurney in the hall where the woman who does the menial stuff left it. She seems to think it's in her contract to be miserable. Between her and the exhausted nurses it's a wonder more doesn't go wrong, with endless prescriptions to keep straight and inscrutable hoses twisting around cables. Mistakes doubtless occur every day, with lucky benign outcomes and unexplained side effects.

New nurses are common on the floor, to the point where Leo can't keep track of them. He sorts them into types, those he *would* sleep with, and those he *wouldn't*. There are regulars and part-timers and floats that cover the two shifts back and forth. Nice and hard and white, they start their shifts bright and reliable. At the bleak end of their twelve-hour shifts you start to see the watery eyes. They struggle with focus, like stale gamblers.

When nurse Agnes comes on shift he recognizes her musical voice over the whispering chaos of the ward. She was the one who caught him coming in, and who escorted him from emergency to recovery, who took him for X-rays and almost lost him in the maze of long corridors on the bottom floor. He can't make out her words, but he can usually tell how she's feeling, whether she's angry or ecstatic, pissed off at some doctor or promoting some new guru whose book is changing her life. A fascinating contradiction exists between her soothing voice and her egocentric interpretations. For the next half hour he listens for its thread.

He falls asleep. He was a valuable piece of junk how many days ago now? He can't remember. He'd never seen anything handled so carefully. They strapped him onto something well made and raced through the streets with an opera singer on the roof. It was a dream whose fragments were sideways and upside-down and backwards. Nothing made sense and yet it made perfect sense. Agnes's voice is nearby. He opens his eyes.

Hi Leo.

He opens his eyes again.

How are you feeling?

How am I feeling? He sighs and his face goes slack because he doesn't understand the question. How does he feel? He doesn't know.

She laughs. She's always laughing at the wrong time.

And that's not the worst of it, he says, trying to align himself to her enigmatic good humour.

According to your chart, you've been bathed, she says.

That must be a mistake. I've been waiting for you to give me one.

It's right here on your chart.

No one does it quite like you.

Why do I get the feeling you're trying to pull a fast one?

Seriously, he says, then forgets what he is saying, falling through a hole in the morphine.

I have an idea.

Oh?

I'm taking a course. You can be my guinea pig.

She holds her hands a few inches above his body and moves them, slowly down one leg and back up the other, over his burnt arms and his scarred face, and then, for a few extra seconds, over his chest and abdomen, where the grafts were harvested from.

It's called healing touch, she says.

But you're not touching.

Can you feel it?

What am I supposed to feel?

Your skin coming to life, your vital organs vibrating.

Define vibrating.

Oblivious to his innuendo, she says, *You are a very fortunate man.*

In the bed opposite is an old man who stares at the ceiling. Leo tried to be friendly once and the poor old thing struggled to raise himself on an elbow, to be friendly back, but lost the battle with gravity and gave up. His wife visits every day and holds his hand and smoothes his hair, patiently threads a thin smile onto his lips.

Leo is watching Agnes as she reads the chart at the foot of the old man's bed. She is talking to his wife, but Leo can't make out the words. On one level what she's saying makes sense. He listens with great care and is satisfied with not understanding anything. He notices Agnes's feet are attached to her wrists, and she is telling the old man that his death has no meaning, that his wife has remarried Leo, but that he shouldn't worry because there was a ham sandwich for him.

Leo wakes up and watches the old man being guided to the bathroom by his wife. Supporting his brittle skeleton is no burden for her, continuing the tasks she has performed at home for many years. He is ancient and has always been ancient. Back into bed she pulls the curtain around the bed and bathes him with a cloth. Their reflection in the window allows Leo to see her linger over his genitals. He wonders what makes their kind of devotion. How was it possible for a human to be so deserving, considering who we have become, considering the times we live in? Marriage was, at its best, a hobby; at its worst, a calling. It was as if love had broken its chains and was terrorizing the city. But the old couple had discovered something more reliable.

Last night it began, the wet, irregular breathing. The old man gasps and wheezes and then goes quiet and Leo wonders if this is it, the silence ballooning until it fills all the available space in Leo's attention. Then an explosion of air begins the cycle over again, each breath a tantalizing plum he could not quite reach. Leo asks the nurse for a sleeping pill and some earplugs. But the pneumonia coiled in the old man's chest would not be shut out.

Leo's mind eventually wanders off during one of the silences. He was playing golf with his uncle David. Leo was twelve and having an exceptional day, scoring his first par round, while Uncle David was a duffer. The physical mysteries of the game left him dazzled. He had a graceful swing and some knowledge of the sport, but he inevitably hooked the ball into the trees. Though he couldn't play the game he was able to teach Leo, with very little deliberation, how to send the ball into a long arc where it seemed to hang in the sky. They cheered each other on, strode together down the fairway, laughing 'til they cried when Uncle David put his ball in the clubhouse parking lot, dinging any number of cars.

In the morning the dead man's wife has drawn a curtain around the bed and is washing the body. Leo wonders at what point a *him* becomes an *it*. Where was the moment? Was it a tight squeeze, or a slow forgetting? People become genderless long before they stop breathing. They give up their passions and wander a barren world of objects. Why did Leo stop seeing his uncle? He didn't really know. After his marriage failed he was too ashamed, too unworthy, too afraid.

Pulling the curtains open, the dead man's wife smiles at Leo, then she leaves without looking back. She seemed absolutely sure of who she was. But given the imbalances, the dreadful mistakes concealed behind our best efforts, how was that possible?

He feels sad, and this angers him. Let the sadness surface as a prayer, he says to himself, not knowing what he means, or who he is talking to. It comes up from the ground, through the floors, and it grabs Leo's insides, turning him into mud. Even his embarrassment is powerless to stop him and he is grateful the dead man has the decency not to look.

Leo is standing on Lasha's porch. He doesn't know what he's doing. The skin grafts on his hands have healed, though his hands look odd and they don't work like they used to. He reaches for the bell but his hand won't twist the right way to make it ring. But the door opens anyway and there she is, in a bright yellow taffeta dress with wide hooped skirts, the geese sitting in a new stroller that stands in the hall.

We were just going out, she says, pulling gloves on up to her elbows.

He doesn't know why he feels so unemotional. He doesn't understand why he came here. It was stupid and he knows it. But he didn't come for her sympathy so he bears up under her scrutiny.

I just came . . . he stammers, because he doesn't know what to stay, *I came to say one thing.*

When she doesn't slam the door in his face, as he was expecting, he relaxes a bit. He's exhausted from walking so far and grateful she hasn't brushed him off.

Thank you . . .

Thank you? she echoes. Of all the apologies and excuses she might have expected, all the nights she had him there in her mind, wondering what he was going to say when he came back and rehearsing what she would say in response, "Thank you" hadn't occurred to her.

By thank you, she asks, *you're telling me . . . what?*

I don't know.

Are you apologizing?

That's not what I meant.

Are you being sarcastic?

Is that how I sound?

You've changed.

She thought she should be angry, and flatly refuse to hear him out, but something was stopping her. She had tragically overestimated her knowledge of men, mis-judged Leo's acuity, overplaying her signals by putting his things out, and she had paid a high price for it.

Walk with us, she says.

Sure.

There aren't many people out at this time of the morning, yet it is difficult to walk beside her on the narrow sidewalk without stepping on her dress, avoid-ing hydrants and sign posts, deferring the right of way to the curious birds.

Any rooms available? he gets up the nerve to ask.

Josephine's old room is empty.

Leo can't read her, doesn't know if this is an assent. He feels a million miles away and getting further by the minute.

Are Stephen and Narayan still there? he asks.

Oh yes.

She stops in the middle of a crosswalk and asks, *Where are your tools?*

We can't stand here, he says, stumped by the question, deferring the truth to some other time. She looks at him quizzically and then moves off across the street. He follows her down the next block, but he's suffering and can't keep up.

It occurs to Lasha what she is doing, though unconsciously, trying to make him suffer. She stops.

Why don't you go back to the house and get some rest, then we'll have something to eat. I think it's Stephen's turn to cook.

Nine

CLEAR-CUT OVERCOMES the road as Stephen drives them up into a slash that runs as far as you care to look. The valley was sold for its shade and now the mountainside is prone to slides. A rock the size of a small car has torn out part of the road on its journey down, seriously damaging Leo's confidence in this trip, which was Lasha's suggestion against his better judgment.

Why do men feel the need to please women? Leo wonders out loud.

Women are gods, Narayan says, *you just have to accept that.*

They have to be appeased, Stephen says.

With flowers, Leo has always thought.

No, with futile second guessing, Stephen says.

The trick is to deny them sex, explains Narayan. *The*

more skilfully you love them, the more irrational they become. It's death to intellectual freedom.

Deny them sex? Leo asks.

At the top of the ridge the road turns into an abandoned operations yard and dust overtakes the truck. Wandering around the oil stained yard, kicking out of the soil a disposable lighter, the tooth from a saw, Leo adjusts his baseball cap.

They unload sheet metal from the back of the truck and Stephen licks his fingers to test the battery.

Leo stands over the explosives and watches Stephen work.

Monobel, Nitroglycerine, ammonium nitrate, and ammonium chloride, holding a stick under his nose like a cigar. *I've used 'em all,* says Stephen. *From gelatines to liquid oxygen. They're all unique.*

Narayan drags a sheet to the centre of the clearing and Stephen sets the charge. They walk backwards to the truck at the pace of the unspooling wire.

You guys ready?

You're sure this is safe? Leo asks.

It's no less safe than a lot of things.

Gravel bullets under the truck between their legs. Leo and Narayan exchange a look.

Leo notices the smell.

Nice, isn't it?

What is it?

The atoms get rearranged.

They fan out into the slash to find it, stand it on edge so Stephen can examine it. The explosion has punched a hole whose jagged horns create a ghastly rose.

The next one lands beside the truck, piercing the ground like a broken bone.

They pause to eat the rice bread sandwiches that Lasha made for them. They crumble in their hands and Stephen and Narayan shake their heads and look at Leo like it's his fault Lasha brought a bread machine into the house. She's been trying out new recipes with different combinations of ingredients, every morning filling the house with the aroma of breads made from potato flour, tapioca, corn.

They blast the remainder of the sheet metal and the mountaintop rings with their exclamations and haloes of dust float in the air. The ground shudders and the air shakes. Fir seedlings in the slash shiver with nervous energy as the men get bolder with each concussion.

With the sun glowing in the west they load up Stephen's new creations, and what's left of his explosives—a few sticks of dynamite and some blasting caps—and drive out just ahead of dusk. The potholes in the road seem deeper and strewn with rocks like pictures of Mars. In places the road has disappeared under the shifting dynamics of the mountainside. It's rough, and barely passable, worse than when they came in, though less frightening having gained the status of the road home. They are expended, their bodies supple, shoulders knocking and knees touching, riding with it.

June's probation officer is a busy man. He works ten-hour days and has lunch at his desk. He's easily distracted by details, shreds of lettuce in the folds of his shirt. June sits there and watches him organize himself for their meeting, their last. He writes something in her file and folds it back into the collapse on his desk. She wonders what he's on. He asks her questions that don't require answers. *How is everything? How are you feeling?* He's like a shrink that way, ineffectual and shooting in the dark. He takes comfort in crossing his T's and dotting his I's.

She never tells him her true thoughts or about her violent impulses, the one to smack him a good one, for instance, when he leans forward in his chair trying to remember what they were talking about.

He's looking at her funny because something is different and he can't figure out what. He doesn't grasp what's staring him in the face, that she isn't wearing make-up today. Leo said she should try it, go a day without to see what it was like. But all she feels is anxious, naked, like a shy teenager. Leo came over after he moved back to the bird woman's house. She meant to ask him where he'd been keeping himself.

How was your week? asks the probation officer.

Same as usual.

This is our last meeting.

Yah?

What are your impressions?

About what?

About the last year. The system. Whatever.

She could tell him she felt like she was in a Kafka novel but he'd misunderstand and take it personally and make a notation on her record. "Difficult. Likes to invoke existentialists." She could tell him her feelings, but in a system that discourages intuition and originality that would be like suicide. Getting ready to end the session, he pats her file and smiles. Soon it will be in the metal drawer where it lives, a job well done.

She could tell him he's just another overweight man whose brain was pulled out through his nose with a coat hanger. She could tell him that he doesn't know a thing about her. All he's got is a file the ministry has on her mistakes, case #1787501-3, a monster with a mean left hook and no tongue. She could try and tell him the truth, and go stumbling into the street, terrifying people and picking up cars. But the truth is a dangerous thing to hand someone who claims to have your best interest in mind.

Come on, tell me what you think, he encourages her. *Off the record.*

I'll tell you one thing, she says, *you're doing a terrific job. You're helping people.*

Yah? he says, still hoping for what he can't have, his expression promising face value.

Yah, she nods. *I think I've learned a thing or two,* she says, rubbing it in that he knows perfectly well she can't afford to trust him.

Unable to persuade her to be his buddy, he offers her his hand.

Good luck, he says.

We all try our best, she offers, with an ironic smile.

Thanks, he says. *I appreciate it.*

June is meeting Rick and Gunther at the park. He offered to take them for lunch, though she knows that at the last minute he'll find an excuse and back out. It's actual currency with him, believing good intentions bought him something. When they started seeing each other she was confused by it, the propositions and broken promises. By the time she realized he was pathologically full of crap, it was too late.

She can see Rick and Gunther playing catch with a softball at the other end of the field. She gets on a swing and gives herself a little push, enjoying the air up her skirt.

The game of catch gets closer as she pumps higher on the swing. When it's the body in motion, can you still call it wind? How intelligent Rick looks; it was a funny thing about good-looking people. If he'd only

learned how to focus it, he might have become something a little more specific.

Rick waves and gets Gunther to wave. June pumps
the swing as high as she can make it go, the chains
going slack at either end of her pendulum. She wonders if it's possible to swing right round without
breaking her neck on the bar? She's always breaking
her neck on the bar. Rick and Gunther scramble onto
swings on either side of her. Gunther twists and
squirms trying to get moving. June stops swinging to
give him a push but he crossly tells her not to.

Fine, she says, annoyed, *do it yourself.*

He's going to be an inelegant ape when he grows
up, a giant child with a vocabulary of five hundred
words. Sturdy as a wall and good for hanging pictures.

Rick looks at her. Was she too sharp with the boy?
Does Rick notice that sort of thing?

You're not wearing make-up, he says.

So?

Why?

It feels good, she lies.

It makes you look like an old woman.

Why don't you shove it?

*Gunther, your mummy isn't wearing make-up.
How does she look?*

Yucky.

They walk back to June's place where Rick suddenly

remembers an important appointment he totally forgot about.

We'll go for lunch some other time, June says.

Okay. Good idea. Gotta go.

June opens a can of soup and later they go shopping. She buys lipstick and eye shadow, trying them first on Gunther because he has her colouring.

Gunther sees Tess as a kind of mechanized grandmother. He can't keep his eyes off her chair. He stands on the pew while June holds his ankle. Tess watches the boy with horror as he unconsciously intertwines his fingers in his mother's hair, making her wince.

The apprentice calls the children to the front and Gunther looks at his mother.

Go ahead, she encourages.

June doesn't think he'll go. But he wants something she can't define; he wants to decide for himself. He gets off the pew and runs down the aisle following the other children.

Do you know what Easter is about, children? the apprentice asks them in a voice meant to carry to the rest of the congregation. *Candy? No, not really. Bunnies? Well, part of it is. But the most important part? Who knows what the most important part is?*

I do find this part ever so interesting, Tess being

sarcastic. *Isn't it fascinating how a grown person can be so inexperienced. Who can blame the minister for preferring the other one.*

But June is interested. What *is* the most important part of Easter? She likes the simple explanations of impossible things, and finds the apprentice's tone reassuring. June is on the dark side of her mood this morning, and Christ is offering to carry it for her. She makes an effort to hand it over, imagines shrugging off her grief like a shawl, but this only worsens her headache. Coming to church this morning was an attempt to structure what was going to be a lost day, one with Gunther trying to create some sound in the void, trying to hurt his mom, to bring her back.

Tess is beautiful this morning. Church gives her an attractive dignity. Maybe that's it, when all else is lost. June tries to imitate it but her headache throbs. And as if that wasn't bad enough, who sits in the pew beside her but Kaslikoff.

What are you doing here?

I came to see for myself.

Came to see what?

Hi there, he says, leaning over June to shake Tess's hand.

You don't go to church, June tells him.

He gives her a look and she shakes her head, introducing them, *Tess, this is Kaslikoff; Kaslikoff meet my friend Tess.*

George, Kaslikoff clarifies for Tess, then he asks her, *How's the stock market treating you?*

Seriously, what are you doing here? June asks him.

Why have you never told me about this one? Tess is beaming.

I've never told you about any of them. And believe me, you don't want to know.

I should have gotten into the market years ago, Tess says, in answer to his question.

Recently June put a thousand of Tess's dollars on a stock and sold it the next day for eighteen-hundred. Now Tess has gold fever and, living in a dream world, is determined to earn enough to take a tropical holiday.

I've tried to explain that it's not so simple, June says, *that every win has a loss, or two, or ten.*

It's all in the touch, Kaslikoff says to Tess.

The touch, yes, of course. It would be.

The apprentice finishes her story and sends the children to the kindergarten. Gunther stays with the group, waving at his mother as he runs by.

A man in a navy suit begins directing the congregation to file to the centre aisle and then proceed to the front in groups of five to take communion.

Have you picked your next one? Kaslikoff asks.

June has some ideas.

The man in the navy suit directs them to stand and they follow Tess. June tells Kaslikoff that he can't take communion but doesn't have an answer when he asks her why. They kneel, one on either side of Tess's motorized chair.

Tess whispers to Kaslikoff, *We just want to make enough for a holiday, so I can go for a proper swim in the ocean.*

Have you ever seen black sand beaches? Kaslikoff mumbles back.

June is mortified.

The minister holds his thumb on her lip for as long as the wafer takes to melt. Then the deacon lifts the silver chalice, wiping the rim with an embroidered silk cloth.

The next sure bet investment they make is on a company called Highnet. June felt good about it based on what she'd read and because Kaslikoff liked it.

It's chomping at the bit, he says. *Tell Tess this is it. No, let me tell her. Put her on.*

Kaslikoff starts coming over to Tess's place with take-out food and whisky. He tells her about herd mentality and the bogeyman, the unknowable elements that drive a good stock into the ground or make a worthless one fly to the moon.

It has a mind of its own, he says, pouring another drink.

It's late in the evening and June had wanted to go home hours ago, but she doesn't want to leave Tess alone with Kaslikoff. It wouldn't be fair to her.

The market is governed by the stars, Kaslikoff says, enlarging his bullshit into a philosophy. *You know it by the shrapnel in your knee. You watch the sky for signals, pay attention to your feelings. You must know the difference between intuition and wishful thinking.*

Tess is hanging on his voice, drinking a few too many herself. His penetrating earnestness seems comical to June.

Is it wishful thinking for me to want to go to bed?

Not at all. Need a ride?

You're in no shape to drive.

He can stay here. Sleep on the chesterfield, George.

What does it feel like to lose? June asks him, deciding to stay a while longer.

You don't want to know, he says.

Tell us, Tess says.

It's not that winning isn't a blast, he says, pausing to contemplate something that put into words sounded impossible and absurd. *It just can't touch the beauty of losing. Winning is like reading good fiction; while losing, on the other had, is more like living it, seeing the world for the first time, for what it is.*

What is it?

It's not what you think.

A few days later Highnet begins an agonizing fall. This was what June hated about the market, that queasy feeling, the regret. You regret it when you sell too soon, or when you sell too late; you regret being bold, cautious or middle of the road. If you make money it's tinged with the regret that if you'd hung on a little longer you could have made enough to retire. A negative news release is apparently responsible, and rumours layer rumours, important points defy the facts.

It's difficult to walk beside Tess when her chair takes up most of the sidewalk. In the coffee shop she bulldozes chairs around to clear a table, while June orders sandwiches and cappuccinos. They talk about Mexico and Barbados, seat sales and airport terminals.

Where are we going to go? Tess asks.

If I don't lose all your money?

I used to swim every day when I had someone to take me.

Back at the computer, June stares at the starfield screen-saver while Tess goes to the bathroom, her skinny arms pushing the wheels of her manual chair. June resigns herself to the irritating succession of noises. The bathroom door is too narrow for the chair, which is why she keeps the walker handy. She stands up, gripping the handholds, and strikes out for the toilet, her bad leg more or less dragging behind her as she pushes a few inches at a time, causing the rubber walker feet to fibrillate on the floor.

The next sound June expects is the "whoops" as she drops the last six inches or so to the seat, the tank lid clanging when she bumps it. Then comes the tinkle and plop. June paws the mouse and squints at the screen, trying to remember what she was doing. But then there's a loud crash and a small cry, and June finds Tess sprawled on the floor with her slacks around her ankles and shit everywhere.

But she can't get past the wheelchair into the bathroom and it won't budge because the brakes are set and in her fluster she can't work the mechanism. It's too heavy to lift, so she drags it backwards, the foot-rests banging side to side into the walls.

Out of breath and kneeling beside Tess, she can't escape the stink of the old woman's excrement.

Are you okay?

I think so.

Did you break anything?

Nothing is broken.

Tess tries to sit up but doesn't have the strength.

What should I do? I'll call 911.

Don't you dare, Tess cries. *They'd take me to the hospital.*

You might be injured.

Oh dear . . .

When does your homemaker get here?

Not 'til dinnertime. I'm sorry dear. I'm terribly sorry.

June pulls Tess's clothes off, trying to contain the dirt, tossing them into the bathtub. June wants to ask how it happened, but it would just make both of them feel worse.

It's going to be fine, she says instead.

She gets behind Tess and takes her in a bear-hug, managing to slide up the wall and get her back onto the toilet seat. She runs a washcloth under the hot water and gives it to Tess. June cleans the floor with towels and tosses them into the tub along with the clothes. Tess is hopeless and June takes over washing, shocked by the skin, so loose and scarred, so abjectly draped on her skeleton. Tess can't lift her arms, so sliding a nightgown over her head is like dressing a doll. June pivots on what little strength the old woman has left and in a kind of waltz gets her to the chair and finally into bed. Tess is contrite and childlike and June doesn't know how to reassure her.

June makes an attempt to clean herself up, but it's pointless. She needs to go home and have a shower. Tess hooks an arm over June's neck and pulls her down for a kiss. She says she will nap until the home-maker comes.

Whatever June may have learned about business over the years vanishes when a critical decision has to be made. Her intuition gets drowned out by hope and doubt and in the end all she has to go on is the almighty guess.

Focus, dear, Tess says, sounding too much like Kaslikoff. *Don't believe the lies, particularly your own.*

Easy for you to say.

She decides to hold on and Highnet bounces back and when June sells they make another minor killing.

A company called Arknet is developing software that can teach itself to recognize meaningless data and automatically delete it. June has a good feeling about this one. And again it pays off.

The next one is Boogynet, one Kaslikoff has dug up that he thinks has incredible potential. June is confident, too confident; it was one of the signs she should know by now, one of the signs that signals she is full of shit. The next day a negative article appears and it starts to slide, and over the next few days it continues to lose ground.

On Friday June wakes up depressed. When she calls Tess to see if she's online yet, Tess excitedly tells her she'd better come over. Boogynet was back up at ninety cents.

Kaslikoff shows up later with a large pizza and a bottle of vodka.

It's like surfing, he says, getting philosophical early, sipping his lunch martini. *The trick is to jump off before the wave breaks, to see the moment before the moment sees you, before it drives into the rocks and takes you with it.*

But how do you know the moment when it comes? Tess asks.

I don't know, he admits, *every trader has her own*

voodoo; be they business fundamentals, tarot cards, or Zen, it doesn't seem to matter. It's how thick your skin is, in the end, that counts for something.

Boogynet is holding steady up around a dollar. If June sells now, they will come out ahead, but only with a small profit.

May said it was going to go a lot higher, June says.

But do you think it'll go higher? Tess insists.

It's going up, Kaslikoff says.

But what about you, June? What do you think?

I don't know.

Think, girl. Grow up.

It shouldn't be as high as it is, June says, stung by Tess's tone.

Well, then . . . ?

But June doesn't trust herself and decides to hold on. And almost immediately it starts down, and by morning disaster has hit. A notice goes up on the web that trading in Boogynet has been suspended while the company is investigated for insider trading.

June doesn't answer her phone for a week.

Ten

R ICK DROPS ONTO the couch and, feeling between the cushions, finds a few coins and some popcorn.

You didn't forget I was coming, did you? he asks her.

No. Why?

I don't know. The way you looked at me. When I came in.

How did I look at you?

Hey, guess what? I got a job.

Doing what?

Working at a desk.

Phone solicitation?

Better, much better.

What?

Debt collection. Are you all right?

Who'd you leave Gunther with?

How'd the thing go with the old lady?

I told you already. I lost her money.

How high did you get it?

You should have seen me Rick, I was in the zone. Hey, feel like making a salad? I need to make a call.

She takes the phone into the other room and Rick starts the salad, pulls vegetables from the fridge.

June comes back smoking a cigarette and puts the casserole she prepared earlier into the oven.

Mind if I put some music on? Rick says.

Have you ever heard of sleep-cooking before? I made a kielbasa the other night.

You don't remember cooking it?

It was the best kielbasa I ever made.

Rick is trying to find a soft rock station playing something heavy, shaking his head at her crazy ideas.

The counter was a mess.

Are you on drugs? he asks.

I've been getting ready for my trip.

She sits down and her skirt goes for a hike and Rick makes no effort to conceal his interest. He slides closer and puts a hand on her knee and leans over and kisses her forehead, tasting her perfume. He slides his hand under the skirt. Her thighs are smooth.

You were the only one for me, she says absently.

Her words remind him of the past, of what happened, of what always happens. Her words sound like some corny soap opera script and he quickly loses interest.

You wanna go for a drive? he asks.

Yah, this is stupid.

He races a yellow light and panic stops at a cross-walk, lurching on when the stunned pedestrian, too frightened to think straight, waves them through.

They drive to Queen Elizabeth Park and go for a walk through the gardens.

Want to get back together? he says.

Yah, right, she laughs.

I know you better than you think.

Okay, but so what?

We could take a nice honeymoon.

I told you, I'm going to Kona.

With that stupid old lady?

Is she old? I hadn't noticed.

You are so lying to me. I thought so.

What are you talking about?

You said you lost that old lady's money, but if that was true then where are you getting the cash for the trip and the cocaine?

Okay, I lied.

I can't believe you'd waste a perfectly good holiday.

June stands on the lookout staring at the quilt of lights over the city, which almost resembles something sleeping. Rick is banging on the Henry Moore sculpture with his open palms, making a sound that doesn't carry far.

Hey June bug, he says, his hands cooling on the bronze, *I'm sorry about all those calls to the ministry.*

We should get back to my casserole.

He goes back to drumming and in the clear night it sounds good and uncomplicated.

Getting back to June's place he leaves the engine running.

You're not coming in? June asks.

There's something I need to do. It's important. I completely forgot about it.

It's the thought that counts.

He drives away and June goes for a walk around the block.

Leo sits cross-legged on the sidewalk, with his back to what used to be a calendar store, some brilliant turkey's big idea. It had strong customer loyalty leading up to Christmas, and for about a week after. Before that, the space was a used bookstore, its shelves stupid with outdated textbooks and military histories. A new tenant hasn't been found yet. Leo feels safe here, no one will tell him to move.

Some days the downtown streets are saturated with beggars, from every crack and corner an outstretched hand, a styrofoam cup, a hat. Buskers suck up the good change, beggars with talent, violins and penny whistles. Occasionally a bum will try to elevate himself—the ventriloquist whose lips move, the junky with the hockey stick trombone. Don't encourage bad actors is what Leo wants to tell them, the couples in love, the generous tourist who has never seen the likes.

Other bad actors include Mary Queen of Scots, after the beheading, Adolph Eichmann begging for clean sheets, John Wayne, all Elvis impersonators, Elvis, the toothless man with the mulberry bush guitar, the two-for-Tuesday cinema centipedes extending around the block.

A classical cellist makes the rounds of the best spots. With her training and her compact body, she is a good one. A red-headed Irishman juggles a baby stroller, an umbrella, and a golf ball. A sword swallower appeared one day, and the next day was the headless man.

Leo's act is three brushes, a chamois, various shades of brown and black polish. He is proud of his boar bristle brushes and cares for them lovingly. All of his equipment folds into a single box he can carry on the bus. He is able to look his customers in the eye if he keeps a tight rein on his moods. He has to be alert and cocksure if he expects anyone to come near him. He has a sign: *Shoes Shined, by Donation.* He watches the sidewalk for the right kinds of shoes, then tries to capture their owner with gentle banter, putting them at ease, drawing them over for a quick shine, thirty seconds per shoe. Into his hat they toss a dollar or two. He can make a hundred on an average Friday, and he pays no taxes. Rabbit is rich.

A group of street kids have made him an honorary friend. He earned their trust by keeping his mouth shut and answering all their questions. *What was Beatlemania like? Explain optimism to us.* And don't expect. Expectations are cages their parents kept them in and the butterfly nets social workers try to catch them in. And missionaries come paddling up-river in their canoes with bibles and blankets; following in their wake, the drug merchants and slavers.

Their leader is a young woman named Jenny who believes that Leo is some kind of medicine man, the possessor of deep knowledge, while he imagines her in pumps and a tight skirt, though the fantasy requires a lot of work. He'd have to get rid of the hardware and the tattoos, and teach her how to stand up straight and be coy.

She shares a cigarette with him, stirred to loyalty because he isn't afraid of her cooties. A former intra- venous drug user, she prefers *talking* to *sex*, which explains her failure at prostitution. She is saddened by this failure to measure up and he wants to give her fatherly encouragement, tell her she could have been terrific.

To grow hair on the palms of your hands, the soles of your feet, he lectures them. *Survival is an interesting problem. It spurs the growth of unexpected things. The past and the future, to discard them, non-refundable empties that they are.*

Jenny listens to him and nods, paraphrasing in her head. "Hope is a dangerous drug," "Happiness is an act you stage for yourself," and "Peace makes war." What's left are small things, a Quarter-Pounder that's still hot, a day without rain, a day with rain.

Getting up early to paint the house, sleep depression sits on him like a brick hat. Ophelia and Little One are in the kitchen to greet him, and go for the grain he scoops into his hand. He enjoys the power-tool feel of their fervour. He strokes Ophelia's neck, alive as an erection, brawny and delicate. Lasha stirs, says something in her sleep, and they go to investigate. One day when she was out he touched her pillow with the back of his hand, and longed to bury his face in the conflux of her unmade bed.

In the basement he slips into coveralls and carries the ladder outside. Morning must be approached in all the right ways, with the proper rituals and a submissive attitude. He returns to the kitchen and boils water for coffee and has a bowl of cereal. The goddess of morning requires two cups.

He stands next to the ladder admiring what he's accomplished so far. But he's careful about those kinds of feelings, one missed step can snowball into a bad day. It wasn't about having confidence. It was about having nothing. He puts his cup on the ground and opens the paint cans.

He goes slowly, savouring the occupied time. The knowledge that he is responsible for his own burdens has made them bearable. A good father is only the sum total of his flaws. Life was a procession of blunders, a constantly changing mind. His mistakes were feelers into the unknown, evolution firing on all cylinders.

At noon he washes his hands in the laundry tub and goes up to sit in the kitchen, listening to the gentle hum of oblivion around him, from the appliances and the forced-air furnace, from Lasha humming as she works on a candle. The hour moving between a half-day's completed work and the half yet to come.

Beeswax permeates the kitchen. He loves to watch it liquify and shimmer in the pan. Lasha is blind to everything else, her hands thinking, her mind like a pool. If he makes an attempt to bring her out, he'll just fall in with her.

Tell me where you're from and who you used to be, he says, after picking wax out of his sandwich.

She looks up. *I like your version,* she says.

He thinks about it and guesses she's right.

Let's see, where were we. You attracted the attention of one of Europe's most famous princes and were

*invited to meet with him after the play, but by the
time you got to his box he was gone, whisked away by
bodyguards. The air raid sirens started, the blackout
curtains came down. You were left alone in the dark,
cavernous theatre.*

Poor creature.

In the afternoon he paints the trim, the curlicues and
the newel posts the colour of Lasha's lips when she
blushes. Leo crosses to the other side of the street to
admire the whole effect. Unaware of him there, the
woman and her birds come home—a paisley chiffon
breeze, bringing with it the trees, the sky.

Flying into Kona airport was, for June, like arriving in
hell. She was so sure of liking the place that the reality
hits like an air pocket. Out of the window all she could
see were lava flows and drab desert. Waiting for the
hotel limousine she stands at the edge of one, baking
like a skillet in an egomaniacal sun. It was a field of
metal alloy, desolate and alien. Nothing could have
survived. Where the highway cut through, people had
spelled out their names in white shells which they carried up from the trunks of their cars. The temperature
swarmed like bees and all the Fords were white.

When they get to the hotel, she sleeps for an hour

and her mood improves. At dusk, the sky becomes a cavernous thing and the horizon's ethereal breathing seems to glow. That night they have a drink in a lounge without walls and watch for manta rays in the floodlit cove below.

They talk to Kaslikoff on the phone and tell him again how much they appreciate what he's done.

Do you like the hotel? he asks.

Service like you would imagine service, Tess tells him.

All you need to do is think a thirsty thought and a waiter appears? he asks bitterly.

You got it! she says.

He was being a good sport about it. It wasn't June's fault he refused to be normal. She admitted it was a pretty classy thing, his agreeing not to come, even though he was paying for the trip.

In the morning Tess and June realize they have a problem. June pushes the wheelchair provided by the hotel across the lawn and down the path that runs next to the black sand beach. The sky in its gaudy blue dome makes everything too bright, even the shadows. Blue umbrellas dot the dustless sand.

I still don't know why George couldn't come, Tess says. *I mean, aside from the fact that he's paying for it all.*

You know, I think he's got the hots for you.

He's too much like yourself, dear, that's why you don't like him.

He's nuts.

In this world you'd be crazy not to be.

I could ask some of the waiters to give you a lift.

I don't want to feel like someone is waiting for me to hurry up.

The beach is long and all June can think about is tomato juice. Sure enough, a waiter appears.

A virgin Caesar, she tells him. *Tess? How 'bout you?*

Tess isn't listening, she's staring at the waves, willing them to come closer, watching them charge up the sand, lose heart and fall back.

Oh, screw it, June says to the waiter, *cancel the virgin Caesar.*

Yes ma'am.

Bring me a real one.

They go around a compound of small sailboats where the wind is making their cables chime.

Is it lack of courage? Tess asks.

If Kaslikoff were here I'd be drinking too much.

True . . . but . . .

I don't know what you see in him, frankly.

You can drown in two inches of water, Tess says.

Oh, Jesus, you can drown in a lot more water than that.

Kaslikoff just needs someone to love.

He's got you hasn't he, June says. *We should find some shade if nothing else.*

On the other side of the compound they find a

launching ramp, a tongue of concrete that leads down into the sinuous waves.

What do you think?

Tess is quiet for a few moments, scanning the horizon. She watches the swimmers and a sailing class pinwheeling around an instructor with a megaphone, whose words sink before they reach the shore.

Fuck the torpedoes, she says. *Isn't that how they'd put it nowadays?*

June begins down the slope, trying to control the chair, though with the increasing slope and the rough cement on her feet, the handles slip from her grasp. Tess accelerates down the ramp and gasps at the unexpected coolness of the water, pushing herself free of the chair.

The waiter comes down the beach with June's drink and a complimentary sun hat. Tess swims tirelessly, flowing with the swell, going from a crawl to the breast stroke. June watches her and sees what Kaslikoff saw from the first, that Tess is younger than all of them. It's not that her flaws aren't mitigated by an element that loves her still, but simply that the horizon swims on its back so it can watch her eyes.

———◆◆◆———